Note to Readers

Although the Harringtons and their friends are fictional, the situations they find themselves in are real. The crash at the beginning of the story actually happened. A prototype of the B-29 crashed during a test flight, causing power outages in south Seattle and killing nineteen workers in a meatpacking plant. Because the B-29 was still top secret, the newspapers did not report the full story at the time.

Collecting paper, metal, and fat was an ongoing part of the war effort. Learning to live without as many sweets was, as well. After two years of war, families were becoming used to the shortages and found other ways to celebrate special events.

Some people in the United States were arrested for spying during the war, and schoolchildren were encouraged to be careful about what they said to others. "Loose lips sink ships" was one of the most famous mottoes of the war. While they weren't actually on the front lines, American citizens felt very much a part of the effort to win World War II.

THE HOME FRONT

Bonnie Hinman

BARBOUR
PUBLISHING, INC.
Uhrichsville, Ohio

For my dad, Floyd Wirts, a World War II veteran, and for my uncles, Hank, Bob, Joe, Ray, Calvin, Wendell, Ole, and Bill, who all served with distinction at home or abroad during the war.

ISBN 1-57748-513-0

Published by Barbour Publishing, Inc , P O Box 719, Uhrichsville, Ohio 44683
http://www barbourbooks com

Member of the
Evangelical Christian
Publishers Association

Printed in the United States of America

Cover illustration by Peter Pagano
Inside illustrations by Adam Wallenta

CHAPTER 1

The Mysterious Fire

"Barb, put that tire down," Eddie ordered his twin. "You can't take that on the bus." His sister struggled with an old tire that was almost as big as she was.

"I don't know why not," Barb said, puffing from the hard work. "This tire is going in my pile of scrap. I found it behind that building, and it's mine." She stopped and pulled her woolen cap down farther over her curly dark hair.

Eddie shrugged and adjusted the basket he carried. It was full of old bicycle tubes and tires and a couple of worn-out rubber boots. They each had a pile of scrap rubber in the alley behind the hotel where they lived. They would divide this basketful between the piles, but they couldn't divide the big tire. It was only a few days before the end of the scrap rubber drive, and each twin wanted to have the most rubber to turn in at the collection center.

"At least hurry up," Eddie said. "Frank and Donnie will be waiting for us." Frank was the twins' older brother, and he and his friend Donnie had let Barb and Eddie tag along for once. It was a school holiday, but the older boys were at a third friend's house working on a school project. Eddie and Barb had begged to be included until Frank had finally said they could come along to look for scrap in a new neighborhood.

"They won't be back at the bus stop yet," Barb said.

Eddie shrugged again. Barb was probably right. Frank and Donnie had said to be back in an hour, and it hadn't been that long yet because he had heard a noon whistle from one of the factories farther south not fifteen minutes ago.

Eddie switched hands with his basket. "I think all the rubber we have at home is enough to make an airplane tire."

"No, airplane tires are a lot bigger." Barb tugged the tire over a curb.

"Not all of them," Eddie said. "There are little ones, too."

"How would you know? You've never been close to an airplane."

"Have so!" Eddie hollered over his shoulder.

"Have not!"

At first Eddie didn't pay any attention to the roar that grew steadily louder, but in seconds the air vibrated with sound. He only had time to look at Barb and see a puzzled look on her face before a huge explosion knocked them off their feet, scattering Eddie's rubber into the street.

He lay on the sidewalk for a second or two, waiting and listening, but nothing else happened. He sat up and looked around. "Barb, are you all right?" His sister sat nearby, still clutching the big tire.

"I'm fine. What on earth was that?"

"I don't know. Some kind of explosion." Eddie jumped to his feet. People poured out onto the sidewalks and street. Everyone looked around and talked excitedly to each other.

"Look," Barb said, "over there." She pointed south.

Eddie saw a billow of smoke drift above the rooftops of Seattle. Something was on fire, and by the looks of the smoke, it was something big. The wail of sirens in the distance soon cut through the babble of talk around the twins.

"It was a plane! I saw it!" a woman yelled as she ran past them toward the smoke.

Eddie and Barb looked at each other. Without a word, Eddie knew what his twin was thinking. Together they shoved Barb's tire and the basket under a bush at the edge of the street and ran toward the smoke with everyone else. The need to meet Frank and Donnie had vanished from their minds.

It was farther away than Eddie expected. The smoke had quickly stained the blue sky overhead gray and filled the air with a nasty smell. The closer they got to the main plume of smoke, the more people crowded the sidewalks. Some stared at the sky, but others hurried along with Eddie and Barb toward the smoke's source.

At last they rounded a street corner and saw a fiery scene. Tall tongues of flame licked at a large building that sat back a little from the street. The fire's heat blew at them, along with smoke and cinders. Off to one side an electrical line dangled from a broken pole. It danced through the air like it was alive, shooting sparks in every direction. Eddie pulled at Barb's arm to stop her. Maybe they were close enough.

"What was in that building?" Eddie yelled. A fire engine rounded the corner and sped past them, siren screaming.

"That lady said it was a packing plant," Barb said. "Where they cut up meat."

"There were probably people in there, working," Eddie said. He swallowed hard. "Do you think they were killed?"

Barb stared at the blazing building. "Maybe," she said slowly.

Moments later a woman ran screaming past the twins. "Alfred! Alfred! Where are you?" In a few moments the woman was out of sight, running toward the fire.

Barb and Eddie stared at each other and then back at the fire. Police cars screeched to a halt in the street followed by military cars. More fire trucks arrived and ambulances followed. It was exciting in a horrible way, and Eddie and Barb backed up a little and climbed on an old bench so they could watch.

It wasn't long before the police moved everyone away from the fire. Eddie and Barb escaped notice for a few minutes, but soon a policeman hollered at them to get down off the bench and move along. They obeyed, but Eddie stopped for one last look at the flames.

In the red-orange glow of the fire, he saw something that he hadn't noticed before. The flames had partly burned up the building, revealing the blackened skeleton of what looked like an airplane. He frowned and rubbed his eyes. How did an airplane get in that building? "Barb, look at that." Eddie pointed at the building. "There, inside. It's an airplane. Or what's left of one."

Barb stared for a moment and then raised her eyebrows. "It is a plane. What's it doing in there?"

"Maybe it crashed," Eddie said. "Remember, right before the explosion there was a roaring noise. Maybe it was that airplane about to crash."

"That's what the first woman was yelling," Barb said.

"I told you kids to move along, didn't I?" The policeman was back and gave them a ferocious look.

"We're going," Eddie said. "Did that plane crash into the building and start the fire?" He pointed at the plane framework, which was even more visible in the fire now.

The policeman didn't even look. "There's no plane. It was an explosion of some kind. Maybe gas. No plane involved." He gave the twins a tiny shove. "Now get a move on. This is a restricted area."

"But I can see the plane shape in the fire," Eddie persisted. "Just look."

"I said there was no airplane," the policeman snapped. "If you two don't hightail it out of here, I'm going to run you in."

At that, Eddie and Barb took off down the sidewalk. In his haste, Eddie didn't see a man who was standing partly in the shadow of a nearby church. He ran right into the large, dark-haired man. The man muttered some words in a foreign language and brushed Eddie off as you might a fly.

"I'm sorry, sir," Eddie began, "I wasn't looking." The man seemed not to hear and continued to stare toward the fire.

The twins ran on for a couple blocks before slowing and then stopping by the side of a building.

"I know I saw an airplane in that fire," Eddie said.

"I saw it, too. Why did the policeman say the opposite?"

"I don't know," Eddie replied. "It doesn't make sense. Let's go find Frank and Donnie."

There was a lot in Eddie's life that didn't make sense these days. The war dragged on and on. He could barely remember what life was like before Japanese bombs dropped out of the sky on Pearl Harbor more than two years ago. His oldest brother, Steve, had enlisted in the army right away and was serving in Europe now. Eddie never told anyone, but sometimes he couldn't remember what his brother looked like. When that happened, he went in the living room to stare at Steve's picture on a table.

The older boys were waiting at the bus stop when the twins arrived.

"Where have you been?" Frank said indignantly. "You two wouldn't notice if the street blew up under you if it meant getting some scrap for your collection."

"Wait until you hear what we saw," Eddie said, ignoring his brother's tone.

"Save it," Frank ordered and jerked his head at the oncoming bus. "Donnie and I were supposed to be back at the hotel by one o'clock to meet the coal delivery truck. You can explain to Mama why we're late." Donnie lived in the hotel, too, and he and Frank both worked there after school and on Saturdays.

Everyone on the bus talked loudly about what they had seen, including the bus driver, who claimed to have snapped some pictures of a mysterious airplane flying low a few moments before the explosion. Not everyone agreed that it was an airplane, but they all had felt the jolt.

"Do you think they heard the explosion at home?" Barb asked as they swung off the bus at the corner near the hotel. "Maybe," Eddie said, "but I don't know how loud it would be this far away."

"We'll find out in a minute." Barb turned into the doorway and bounded up the stairs that led to the lobby of the hotel. The twins' family was running the hotel for some Japanese friends, the Wakamutsus, who had been sent to an internment camp soon after the war began. Frank and Donnie ran for the back stairs to see if the coal delivery truck had come yet.

"Why is it so dark in here?" Eddie asked. The only light shone dimly through the windows at the front of the lobby.

"The lights aren't on." Barb walked over to a wall switch and flipped it, but nothing happened.

Their mother rushed out of the hotel office door. "There you are! I've been worried sick. What with the explosion and no electricity, I was thinking awful thoughts." She pulled the twins close for a hug. "Is Frank with you?"

Barb nodded and pointed toward the back of the building.

"Why on earth didn't you come home right away after that explosion? And don't tell me you didn't hear it. Everybody for miles around heard it."

Eddie looked at Barb. He knew what she was thinking. How much should they tell? They would never lie to their mother, but some things were best left unsaid. Barb raised her eyebrows a hair and gave the tiniest of shoulder shrugs. Eddie figured that meant Barb thought they should tell the whole truth because Mama would find out anyhow.

"We were there," he said finally.

"What do you mean?" Mama asked. She sounded suspicious.

"I thought you were collecting rubber in the neighborhood."

"Oh, we were collecting rubber," Barb said. "Just not in the neighborhood. Frank and Donnie took us with them."

"We were right near the explosion," Eddie blurted out. "There was an airplane in the fire."

"But the policeman said it wasn't an airplane," Barb said.

"Only it was," Eddie said, "because we both saw the shape of it in the fire."

Barb nodded vigorously. "We think a plane crashed into that building and caused the fire."

"But we don't know why the policeman said it wasn't a plane," Eddie concluded.

Mama looked in stunned silence from one twin to the other. "You mean to tell me that you went out of our neighborhood without telling me and then saw this fire or plane crash or whatever it was?" she said at last. She stood in the middle of the lobby with her arms crossed, frowning at the twins, who at nine years old were the youngest of the Harrington children.

"We didn't see the crash," Eddie said. "We heard it. It was afterwards that we saw the fire." He avoided the first part of her question.

"And the plane," Barb added.

"Don't tell me another thing right now," Mama said and threw up her hands. "I don't want to know. You children will be the death of me yet." She strode back to the office. "For now get busy and find some extra candles. We don't know how long the power will be off, and our hotel guests will be needing light."

Eddie sneaked a grin at Barb. Off easy so far. Maybe Mama would get busy and forget the whole thing.

Barb grinned back and started down this hall toward their apartment.

"Oh, and by the way." Mama stuck her head back out of the office. "You haven't heard the last of this little episode."

The twins groaned at the same time.

In a few minutes they were in the depths of a storage closet looking for candles. It was hard to do since it was dark in the small room.

"I was sure I saw some candles in here somewhere," Barb said.

"You feel in the boxes on one side, and I'll do the other." Eddie shoved the closet door wide open to get any bit of light from the hallway.

"I don't much like putting my hands into places I can't see first," Barb said.

"Well, just do it," Eddie ordered. "We're in enough trouble anyway. I guess it wasn't such a great idea to go with Frank and Donnie today." He felt among the boxes and other things stored on shelves.

"It was a good idea," Barb insisted, "but the wrong time."

"I'll say."

"Hey, I forgot," Barb said. "We didn't stop and get our rubber and my tire."

"Forget about that stuff. We can get more." Eddie knocked a box off the shelf, but there was no sound of breaking so he felt for it on the floor and shoved it back on the shelf.

"Of course you'd say that," Barb muttered in the dark. "Since it was my tire we left behind. Well, I'm not forgetting. Tomorrow I'm going after it."

"We probably won't be let out of the apartment for a month," Eddie said and fumbled in yet one more box. "We'll probably be on bed detail."

"Yuck! I hope not. I hate changing sheets."

"Here it is!" Eddie yelled. The pieces of candle felt smooth to the touch. The small box was half-full of assorted old and new candles. He tucked it under his arm and walked into the hallway with Barb close behind. Maybe Mama would be so happy to have the candles that she'd go easy on them for leaving the neighborhood. It was more likely that he'd be changing dirty sheets, and the hotel never ran out of that item.

Chapter 2

Mr. Lazarini's Cousin

"A man said in the grocery store that it was a Japanese airplane trying to bomb the Boeing factory but it missed," Barb said as she threw more dirty sheets on the pile in the hallway the Saturday after the crash.

Eddie shoved some of the sheets into a basket. "Dad has always said that Japanese planes couldn't come this far." He remembered the early days of the war when everyone was terrified that Japanese airplanes would swoop out of the sky just like they did at Pearl Harbor in Hawaii. Dad and Mama made sure that the hotel met all blackout restrictions in case of attack, but Dad still said that the Japanese couldn't fly the big bombers nearly this far. Dad was an engineer, so Eddie thought he

15

should know. "I heard a clerk say that an enemy agent blew up the meatpacking plant."

Barb shook her head. "He wasn't a very smart agent if that's what he thought was most important to blow up. Why wouldn't he blow up the shipyards or Boeing?"

"Don't talk about blowing up Boeing. Dad says he and Isabel are safe as can be working there."

"Maybe he just doesn't want us to worry," Barb said.

Eddie frowned at his sister and jammed more dirty sheets in the basket. He handled a lot of his worries by keeping busy and thinking about other things, but it was hard to ignore the fact that his father and sister worked in an important airplane factory. It made sense that the enemy would want to get rid of a factory that helped the United States so much.

"It was an airplane crash, not a bomb," Eddie said firmly. "We saw that with our own eyes. And I don't think it was a Japanese plane, either." Eddie was having a hard time forgetting that fiery scene from the other day. He kept thinking about the woman who had called out for someone named Alfred. Maybe Alfred had died and left his wife and children to take care of themselves.

Eddie knew one thing for sure about war. It meant death—and plenty of it. He couldn't walk a block from his home in the hotel without seeing a gold star in a window showing that a soldier from that family had been killed. Somehow the disaster he had seen last week seemed worse, maybe because it was so close to home. Each night right after he prayed for Steve, he prayed for the families of the people who had died in the fire. He hoped God was listening.

"It must have been one of our planes," Barb said after she

tossed some wet towels into another basket. "But why would the government make such a secret of it? Planes have crashed around here before, and everyone knew."

"I don't know," Eddie said, "but I'm going to ask Dad about it again." The mystery of the plane in the fire was a puzzle he'd like to solve.

"He won't tell you anything." Barb started pushing the heavy basket down the hall.

Eddie sighed as he picked up his own overflowing basket. Dad probably wouldn't tell anything he might know about the crash. He was always quoting the war poster that said *Loose Lips Sink Ships*. Dad said keeping quiet about war production, especially airplanes, was a serious matter. Eddie understood, but that didn't keep him from being curious. Maybe his best friend, Warren, had heard something. They could talk after the Boy Scout meeting that afternoon while they hauled their crushed tin cans to the collection center. If he weren't on double duty here at the hotel because of their rubber-collecting expedition, Eddie would already be out with Warren going door to door, asking for tin cans. This hotel work was never-ending.

"Are we done yet?" Barb asked after the last basket of dirty sheets and towels had been piled in the laundry room.

"No and I want to get everything done before my Boy Scout meeting. There's a new Roy Rogers western playing at the Imperial Theater. Warren and I are going later if I can get my chores done."

"Maybe Carolyn and I will do that, too," Barb said. "But I'd rather see Clark Gable than any old western."

"Get the buckets then. All we have left is scrubbing the hall floor."

17

Barb ducked back into the laundry room, muttering as she went. Eddie followed her and grabbed the mops off the rack where they hung. They were small mops, or Eddie and Barb couldn't have managed them at all. In a few minutes they had partly filled two buckets with cleaner and water from the faucet over the laundry-room sink.

Eddie set his bucket down in the hallway and stared at the faded linoleum floor. "How does this get so dirty?" There were muddy footprints down one side of the hall and a spot or two that looked sticky.

"I don't know," Barb answered. "You wouldn't think people could get their feet so dirty when it hasn't rained for days." She set her bucket down beside Eddie's.

"It will take forever to get this clean," Eddie said.

"I've got an idea." Barb raised her eyebrows. "Let's race. We'll each start at opposite ends of the hall, and the one who gets to the middle first wins."

Eddie eyed the long hallway. Usually they helped their mother or oldest sister Alice mop, and that meant that it took forever since they both insisted on a careful washing and rinsing of the floor. He had often thought mopping could be done in less time, and he was sure he could beat Barb. After all, she was short and skinny and would have a hard time using even the small mop.

"Let's go!" Eddie yelled. He grabbed his bucket and mop and scurried for the far end of the hall. He mopped feverishly, but still his progress toward the middle seemed turtlelike. It took a long time to rinse and wring out the mop every few minutes. Before long his shirtsleeves were soaked with dirty water. There must be an easier way to do this.

The first and second time that Eddie glanced down the hall at his sister, she was about as far from the middle as he was, but the third time he looked, she was much farther along. He stretched his neck to get a better view. She had abandoned her mop and was scooting along on her knees, scrubbing at the floor with a brush and some rags. And was she ever going fast!

Eddie frowned. He wasn't about to let his twin beat him in this race. He looked at the stretch of floor in front of him. The part that took so long was the wringing out of the mop. Maybe he should stop wringing it out. He poured a little of the water on the tile, rubbed it around, and moved on. The water flew as he tried to go faster and faster. He slopped and mopped, slopped and mopped. Before long the hall floor behind him glistened with a sheen of water. Maybe too much water, he thought when he glanced back, but it would soon dry.

Barb sped up, too, but Eddie could see that he was gaining on her. Gaining that is, until a tall blond-haired woman flung open the door to her room and stepped into the hall. She slipped on the wet floor but was able to catch herself by grabbing at Eddie. He promptly staggered into his bucket, dumping the contents. Eddie and the woman stared as the water spread out before them in a tiny tidal wave.

Mama picked that moment to walk around the corner. "What in the world is going on?" The water lay in a big puddle.

"Um, we're mopping," Eddie said and held out his mop for proof. Barb inched around the edge of the puddle to stand by her brother.

"That's not what I would call this," Mama replied crisply. She stared down the hallway. "It looks like you poured water and sloshed it around."

19

Eddie remained silent. The blond-haired woman smiled at him and tiptoed through the water to the lobby with Mama apologizing the whole time.

"Now you two get this cleaned up. Pronto."

"I didn't do it," Barb protested, but Mama gave her a look that made her be quiet.

"Barb didn't do it," Eddie said with a shake of his head. "I managed it all by myself."

"I'm glad you're honest, but she can still help clean up," Mama said and raised a hand to keep Barb from talking. "Experience with you two has shown me that if one is in trouble, the other one usually has something to do with it."

Barb sighed and leaned over to pick up Eddie's bucket.

"I'm off now to volunteer at the ration board," Mama said. "This hallway better be shining clean and dry when I return."

"It will be. I promise," Eddie said. The twins spent the better part of the next hour mopping and wiping and polishing. Eddie thought the floor had never looked so good.

He barely had time to get cleaned up and changed into his Boy Scout uniform before Warren arrived. They always walked to the meetings together, carrying burlap bags of crushed tin cans that they had collected since the last meeting. Sometimes they made another stop or two, looking for cans to fill their bags to the very top. Their troop was way ahead of most of the other troops in Seattle in the amount of scrap they had collected.

"How much tin do you think it takes to make an airplane wing?" Warren asked as they loaded their bags of crushed cans into Eddie and Barb's wagon in the alley behind the hotel.

"More than we have here, that's for sure," Eddie replied.

"More than they had at the collection center last week after we took all our cans?"

"Probably," Eddie said. He grabbed the handle of the wagon and pulled, while Warren pushed and steadied the wobbly bags. They had gone only a few feet when Eddie stopped short. "Wait, I forgot to get Mr. Lazarini's cans. He always has some." The older man lived in a small apartment in the hotel just like Eddie and his family.

"You go," Warren said. "I'll watch our cans. We don't want any Girl Scouts stealing them," he said with a grin. The Girl Scouts collected tin cans, too, and Eddie and Warren were always teasing Barb and her friend Carolyn, saying that the boys could collect more than the girls could.

"I'll be right back," Eddie promised. Mr. Lazarini's apartment was small with only a living room and bedroom and tiny bathroom. He cooked on a little stove that sat right in his living room. In spite of being small, Mr. Lazarini's home was overflowing with plants and flowers that he grew in pots. It was a cheerful, sunny place just like Mr. Lazarini himself.

"It's my friend Eddie," Mr. Lazarini boomed as soon as the apartment door swung open. Out of the room drifted the scratchy sounds of a record player. Mr. Lazarini had been born in Italy and loved Italian opera, which he played endlessly on his old record player. Mr. Lazarini was an American citizen now, and his son was serving in the Pacific with the navy. That left him with no family any closer than New York City. "What can I do for you? Or perhaps you came for a little visit and a bite of biscotti?"

"Sounds great, but I have to get to my Boy Scout meeting," Eddie said. Mr. Lazarini made wonderful treats that he liked to share. Even Eddie's mother was amazed at what the man could cook in spite of all the food shortages and rationing. "Do you have any tin cans for crushing?"

"Indeed I do have some for you." He bustled over to a cabinet, pulled out a paper bag, and handed it to Eddie. "I washed them and took off the bottoms, but I left the crushing to you." He grinned at Eddie.

"Thank you, Mr. Lazarini," Eddie said. His neighbor knew that the boys liked to jump on the cans and flatten them, so Mr. Lazarini always left his cans intact. "I better go."

"Oh, by the way. I'm expecting an air raid warning drill any night now, so be ready," Mr. Lazarini said. Eddie's neighbor was the air raid warden for the block where the hotel sat. He was in charge of making sure that everything went smoothly during the drills. He took his duties very seriously and more than one resident on the block had received a lecture from him when their blackout curtains weren't closed properly. Any light showing outside a house or apartment was forbidden when the air raid sirens sounded.

Eddie had just turned to leave when Mr. Lazarini's bedroom door burst open. A large man stood there with his dark hair going every which way. Eddie stared in puzzlement because the man looked so familiar.

"I'm trying to sleep. First it's that caterwauling music and now you're having a party out here. Can't you keep it down?"

Mr. Lazarini shook his head and smiled broadly. He seemed unconcerned at the stranger's words or his sudden appearance. "I'm glad you're awake, Sal. You can meet my friend Eddie. His family is running this hotel for the owners, the Wakamutsus."

Mr. Lazarini turned to Eddie and explained, "This is my cousin, Salvatorio Bolella."

"So Japs own this hotel, huh," Sal said and nodded at Eddie.

"They are Japanese Americans," Mr. Lazarini said. Eddie saw a hint of fire in the old man's eyes. "The same as we are Italian Americans."

"Right," Sal said, but Eddie had the feeling that Sal only said what he knew was expected of him. Eddie tried to be polite, but he wanted to stare at Mr. Lazarini's cousin. Where had he seen this annoying man before?

"Sal just arrived in Seattle today from New York City. He has come to work in the shipyard and will live with me until he can find his own place." Mr. Lazarini's smile had returned. "It's good to have someone to cook for again."

The cousin's sleep-lined face perked up. "Speaking of cooking," he said, "can a guy get some food around here?"

"Coming right up," Mr. Lazarini said and bustled over to his kitchen area.

After a quick good-bye, which Sal ignored, Eddie escaped with his cans. He frowned as he hurried downstairs to the alley. He must be mistaken about Sal looking familiar if the man had just arrived in Seattle today.

Warren sat on the back step, but he stood when Eddie burst out the door. Something flashed through Eddie's brain, and he remembered where he had seen Mr. Lazarini's rude cousin. Sal Bolella was the man he had run into after the plane crash. He was the man who had mumbled foreign words and then ignored Eddie. But that was days ago. Why had he told Mr. Lazarini that he had only arrived today? Why was he lying? There was something fishy going on with that fellow, but what?

CHAPTER 3
Sliding into Trouble

Warren was all ears when Eddie told him about Sal and his claim to have arrived in Seattle just that morning. In fact, Warren was all for marching right back up the stairs to demand the truth from Mr. Lazarini's cousin.

Eddie shook his head at that idea. He wasn't sure what to do, but facing Sal right now didn't appeal to him. All during the Scout meeting Eddie kept thinking about the stranger. Could he have mistaken Sal for some other dark-haired man?

At last the meeting was over, and the Scouts gathered up their sacks and boxes of cans to cart off to the collection center. Eddie and Warren joined the parade with their wagonload and cheered with the others as the pile of crushed cans towered higher.

"I still think that's enough tin for an airplane wing," Warren said. The friends stood back a little from the pile. "Don't you?"

Eddie didn't answer.

"Eddie, don't you?" Warren repeated and shook his friend's arm.

"Oh, sorry," Eddie replied. "I was thinking about something else."

"Are you thinking about that Sal character? I still think we should go right up to him and ask him why he lied." Warren put the empty sacks in the wagon and grabbed the handle.

"I've thought and thought, and I'm positive that it was him last week." Eddie shoved his hands in his pockets and walked beside Warren, who pulled the wagon. Eddie had always been able to remember faces better than anyone else in his family, and this time was no exception.

"So let's go find him," Warren insisted.

"No, if he's up to something, it might scare him off," Eddie said. "We'll just keep an eye on him. See what we can find out."

"How will we do that?" Warren asked.

"He lives in the hotel. Shouldn't be too hard."

Eddie was still working extra at the hotel, so it was Wednesday after school before he got a chance to check up on Sal and Mr. Lazarini. Wednesday was the day that Barb and Eddie usually collected waste fat from people who lived in the hotel's apartments. Eddie thought it was the worst smelling job of the war, but the fat could be used to make ammunition. He held his nose when possible and reminded himself that these bullets might save Steve.

The twins took turns carrying a big can into which people

dumped their smaller cans of collected fat. After they made their rounds, they took the nearly full can of fat to the butcher's shop, which was the official collection center. At least that was what they used to do. Barb had decided last week that she and Carolyn would collect fat themselves. That way they could contribute the pennies they were paid for the fat to their Girl Scout troop's war bond fund.

So today Eddie was collecting on his own, which suited him fine. That way he could visit with Mr. Lazarini and find out more about Cousin Sal.

"Mr. Lazarini," Eddie called after knocking on his neighbor's door. It would be unusual for the older man to be gone this time of day, but there was no answer to Eddie's repeated knocking.

He was just about to turn and leave when the door opened. The older man peeked out and opened the door wider when he saw Eddie.

"I came to collect your fat," Eddie said. "Just like usual." Eddie waited for the usual jovial response from his friend, but Mr. Lazarini's tired-looking face barely creased into a smile.

"Oh, yes," Mr. Lazarini said. "I forgot this was Wednesday. Come on in, Eddie." He shuffled over to the stove.

Eddie looked curiously at Mr. Lazarini. He had never known the neighbor to forget any detail. In fact, his memory and love of details had earned the old gentleman some teasing, which he seemed to enjoy.

"Where's your opera?" Eddie asked. The apartment was quiet, too quiet for Eddie's taste. He didn't understand a word of the operas that Mr. Lazarini played on his record player, but he liked the sounds and the way Mr. Lazarini would occasionally burst into song, singing along with the record.

"It was too loud for Sal. He works the night shift at the shipyards. Besides, I was getting tired of the same old music."

Eddie couldn't keep his eyebrows from rising to meet his bangs. Mr. Lazarini, tired of opera? That didn't seem possible. "Are you all right?" In his surprise Eddie blurted out the question.

At last Mr. Lazarini gave his normal deep rumbling laugh and put his hand on Eddie's shoulder. "I'm just fine. Maybe a bit tired, what with the new routine. You know, Sal being here and him needing to sleep in the daytime. It's a change, but I'll be fine." He carefully poured his can of grease into Eddie's larger can. "There you go."

"Does Sal like his new job?" Eddie asked. Maybe this was the time to get a little more information about the mysterious cousin.

"I think so," Mr. Lazarini said. "He hasn't said otherwise."

"Did he work in a shipyard back East?"

"I'm not sure. We haven't talked too much about that yet." Mr. Lazarini put his empty can back on the stove.

"Now you have family here again," Eddie said.

"Yes, I do like that," Mr. Lazarini said. He shook his head, and his smile faded briefly. "Sal's not much like the rest of my family, but he needs a place to stay."

Before Eddie could ask any more questions, the bedroom door opened to reveal Sal dressed for work in dark blue pants and shirt.

"Well, well, if it isn't our little chatterbox from the other day." Sal smiled at Eddie, but it wasn't the kind of smile that made Eddie want to smile back. "You're still collecting, I see. What is it this time?"

"Fat for making ammunition," Eddie responded and held up his can.

Sal reached for a pair of gloves lying on the table and jammed them in his pocket before answering. "All this collecting of everything is a waste of time. You can't tell me that some poor sap's leftover bacon grease is worth anything. All those piled-up newspapers and tin cans are just as worthless. The government is sure pulling the wool over your eyes, boy."

"They do so use that stuff," Eddie said loudly. "My father said that fat makes glycerin, which helps make ammunition. He says that if we didn't collect all that scrap rubber and tin cans and such, his job designing airplanes would be much harder. He would have to design them to use less metal and rubber, and that would be really hard." Eddie sputtered to a stop and frowned at Sal.

"So your father designs airplanes at Boeing, does he?" Sal asked. "That's interesting."

Eddie's face felt warm, and he had a sudden urge to bolt out the door. "I can't say exactly what he does. He works in a factory, that's all." Now he'd done it. The last thing he should do was tell a stranger that his father designed airplanes at Boeing. That kind of talk was downright dangerous. Sal had been so aggravating, saying what he did about the collections, but still, Eddic knew that nobody was supposed to talk about war-related factories.

Sal chuckled in a mean way and pushed out the door. He leaned back in to say, "You'll have to tell me more about your father's job when we have the time."

Eddie wanted to sink out of sight through the floor, he felt so guilty.

"Don't mind him," Mr. Lazarini spoke up, "he's just kidding." The old man walked over to his record player and turned it on. The opera he had so recently said he was tired of began to play. In a moment Mr. Lazarini broke into song himself.

Eddie had to grin in spite of all the rotten feelings churning around inside him. His friend seemed restored to his old self. What had made the change? In a couple minutes, Eddie began to feel better himself. Maybe Sal had just been teasing, and after all, everyone in the neighborhood already knew that Father worked at Boeing. Maybe he hadn't done anything that was so awful, but he knew that he would be more careful in the future. And he knew there was more to find out about Sal.

It was almost five o'clock by the time Eddie left Mr. Lazarini's apartment with his can of fat. He'd have to hurry to make his last few stops and still get to the butcher's shop before it closed. No matter what Sal said, Eddie knew that it was important to collect fat and scrap metal and rubber. Finally he was finished, except for Mrs. Hunter. He and Barb always left that neighbor for last because she was often cross and made it seem like they were making large sums of money by selling her small amount of grease. Eddie paused in the hallway. With much arguing, Eddie and Barb had divided up the neighbors when she decided to collect fat on her own, but Mrs. Hunter hadn't been assigned to either.

After some thought, Eddie went toward Mrs. Hunter's door. Before he could knock, Barb and Carolyn appeared behind him.

"Wait a minute," Barb said. "Mrs. Hunter is ours." She carried a can that Eddie could see was almost full of fat. It was fuller than his was by an inch or two.

"Who says?" Eddie challenged and stepped in front of Mrs. Hunter's door.

"I say so," Barb said and shoved up closer. "We divided up these apartments."

"We forgot Mrs. Hunter," Eddie said, "and I got here first. So I get her fat."

"That's not fair," Barb said. "Is it, Carolyn?" The other girl looked unsure but shook her head.

"You already have your can almost full," Eddie said, trying a different approach with his twin. "If I get hers, we'll be even." It wasn't that the fat was so important to him, but lately Barb always had to win everything. It seemed like she was usually one step ahead of him, too. But not this time. That can of fat that Mrs. Hunter saved on the back of her counter was his, fair and square, and he meant to have it.

"We have more in our can because we worked harder," Barb said. "We even went down the street to two other places."

"That wasn't part of the deal," Eddie said. "We just divided up our old route."

"Carolyn and I made the route bigger, that's all."

Mrs. Hunter's apartment door flew open. The middle-aged woman stood, frowning, with her hands on her hips. "What is all the ruckus out here? You children are as noisy as a herd of elephants."

"We came to collect your fat." Eddie and Barb spoke at the exact same time and then gave each other dirty looks.

"Well, why didn't you say so instead of standing out here snipping at each other?" Mrs. Hunter disappeared into her apartment without inviting them in and reappeared shortly, carrying a small tin. "I should be turning this in myself," she grumbled. "Heaven knows, I could use the money. You children probably spend the money on bubble gum."

"No, ma'am," Eddie said. "All of the money goes to buy war bonds or stamps." He wanted to say more but didn't. As if there was any bubble gum to be bought with the few pennies the fat brought. He hadn't had a piece of gum since Christmas, and before that it had been months. The sugar shortage took care of that.

"Here, I'll take that," Barb said and put out her hand to take Mrs. Hunter's can. At the same time she handed her can to Carolyn.

Eddie turned sharply toward his sister to protest, causing his grip to slip on his own greasy can. He jerked his other hand up to steady it and bumped Carolyn, who had been leaning forward to take Barb's can. She in turn lurched into Barb.

In a blink all three cans were airborne. The oily contents squirted everywhere, including down the front of Mrs. Hunter's housedress. The cans clattered to the hall floor, spewing more fat when they hit.

All was silence for a split second, and then Mrs. Hunter shrieked.

"You horrible children," she yelled after catching her breath.

Doors in the hallway popped open as tenants checked on the source of the commotion. On seeing Mrs. Hunter, most of them retreated without a word.

Eddie couldn't move. Fat dripped from his hair to his nose to his shirt. He stared at Barb, who had a big glob of grease slowly sliding down her cheek. Carolyn had escaped the worst of the flow and stood with greasy hands outstretched. It looked to Eddie like she was trying hard to keep from laughing but was about to fail.

Mrs. Hunter continued to complain loudly about ungrateful, ill-behaved, modern children as she backed into her apartment and slammed the door behind her. Eddie looked at the pool of fat on the floor. What should he do now?

That problem was solved when Frank and Audrey walked up, keeping a safe distance from their slippery younger brother and sister. At thirteen, Audrey was a year younger than Frank and the next oldest in the Harrington family after the twins.

"How in the world did you manage this?" Frank asked through laughter.

"Pee-uu," Audrey said while holding her nose, "that stuff stinks."

"Oh, be quiet and hand us some rags and the mops," Barb said, speaking for the first time. She stepped forward but slipped and fell. Eddie reached out to catch her but then slipped, too.

In a flash they both landed on the floor in a tangle of arms and legs. Eddie looked at his sister, whose nose ended up only a foot away from his. That nose glistened in the light, and her hair looked like a wet mop. He knew that he must look the same. He heard a muffled sound and looked at Barb again. She was laughing. He wanted to be mad at her, but he couldn't, not when she laughed like that. So he did the only thing he could do. He laughed, too.

CHAPTER 4

The Secret Weapon

It took the twins and Carolyn a long time to scrub the hallway floor clean of grease. After they finished, Mama insisted that they take their share of a rare batch of cookies to Mrs. Hunter as a peace offering. Eddie hated to miss the cookies, but Mrs. Hunter's stern face relaxed a great deal when he handed her the plate.

In the end, the whole mishap was almost worth the trouble,

because it made a great story to write to Steve. Audrey included the whole tale in a letter she wrote to their brother, reading it to the twins before she stuffed the thin sheets into an envelope.

Eddie was worried about Steve. Every day the newspapers carried bad news about the war in Europe, and radio announcers sounded mournful as they reported German U-boat attacks on American ships in the Atlantic Ocean. They hadn't had a letter from Steve in weeks.

By the end of March, Mama turned pale every time they heard the bicycle bell of the telegram messenger. Her volunteer work at the rations board brought her into contact with too many people who had received the dreaded telegrams announcing that a soldier was injured or missing or, worst of all, killed in action.

The family knew little about Steve's exact whereabouts, but they knew he was in North Africa with a tank unit. Eddie and Barb sometimes talked to each other about their big brother and how scared they were for him, but to Mama they gave only smiles and hugs. When Eddie was especially worried, he went down the street to the mission and sat in the back of the little chapel. He prayed for Steve and all the other soldiers. Eddie knew that he could pray anywhere, but the quiet of the chapel soothed his fears.

Eddie and Barb were busy with school and war efforts and the endless work at the hotel. Eddie usually had so much work to do that he could push his worries about Steve to the back of his mind.

Sal still lived with Mr. Lazarini, but he wasn't around the hotel very much. Everyone else seemed to think he was just a little rude, but Eddie thought it was more than that. Eddie kept an eye on Sal whenever he could. You couldn't be too careful during wartime.

Eventually Sal changed to the day shift, and Mr. Lazarini went back to his opera-singing, cheerful self. Having Sal gone in the daytime seemed to suit him, although he never complained.

April arrived, and with it came spring as well. Mother said the twins must have spring fever, since they argued and fought with each other so often. Eddie tried to ignore his sister when she was bossy, but sometimes he just had to argue with her.

That arguing landed him on the front stairs of the hotel with a bucket of cleaner and scrub brush one Saturday morning. Mama had banished him to the steps and Barb to the laundry room to fold towels. The sun was shining outdoors, and the street bustled with activity. He'd rather be playing baseball with Warren, but if he had to work, this wasn't so bad.

"What's this? Have we a new scrubwoman here? I guess I should say scrub boy." Aunt Daisy's voice interrupted Eddie's vigorous scrubbing.

The Harringtons called their neighbor Aunt Daisy even though she wasn't really their aunt. With all their relatives back in Minnesota, it was fun to pretend that the kind woman was truly an aunt. Aunt Daisy had moved to the hotel last fall after her son, Raymond, shipped out to the Pacific.

Eddie leaned back to grin at her. "I'm in trouble again."

"Surely not," Aunt Daisy said. "Not you or that lively sister of yours, if I were guessing."

"It was all Barb's fault," Eddie began.

"Don't want to hear it," Aunt Daisy said and held up her hand. "I don't doubt there's plenty of blame to go around. What you two need is a new project, and I have had an idea."

Eddie jumped to his feet, sending the scrub brush tumbling down the steps. Aunt Daisy always had great ideas. Sometimes it didn't seem like she thought like an adult at all. "What is it?"

"First we have to find Barb," Aunt Daisy said. "Do you know where she is?"

Eddie nodded. "She's in the laundry, but I'm not supposed to get within ten feet of her."

Aunt Daisy shook her head in mock despair. "Your poor mother has had all she can take, I see."

"I think so." Eddie smiled again, but this time it was sheepish.

"You keep scrubbing while I talk to Lydia. Maybe we can give her some relief."

Eddie scrambled to pick up his scrub brush while Aunt Daisy went in the hotel entrance. He finished the stairs as fast as possible and toted his bucket back inside. He could see Aunt Daisy and Mama in the hotel office near the front door. Both women were laughing, which Eddie took to be a good sign. In a minute Aunt Daisy came out, gestured to Eddie to follow, and walked across the lobby and down the hall to the laundry room.

Barb was stacking clean towels on a shelf when Eddie and Aunt Daisy entered. She looked surprised to see them but very glad to be interrupted.

"Barb, I want you and Eddie to come with me. I have a new project in mind, but I'll need your help," Aunt Daisy said before turning and marching back toward the stairs. She seemed to take for granted that Eddie and Barb would follow. Barb gave Eddie a questioning look, but he could only shrug his shoulders to show that he didn't know what Aunt Daisy was up to, either. The twins hurried to catch up to their neighbor, who had already disappeared down the stairs so recently scrubbed by Eddie.

Aunt Daisy led them down the sidewalk past the second-hand store and the barbershop and around the corner by the cigar shop. They trailed behind her until she stopped abruptly in the middle of the next block. "Here we are," she announced and spread her arms wide.

Eddie looked around in confusion. They stood in front of the vacant lot where he and Warren and Frank and some other kids played baseball. A building had burned there years before and never been rebuilt. The grass was sparse, but the ground was level and made a pretty good baseball field. Across the street were the butcher shop and a dry goods store.

Barb was the first one to speak up. "What do you mean?" She looked as puzzled as Eddie felt.

Aunt Daisy laughed and waved her hand at the lot. "It's perfect for a Victory garden. In fact, there's room for a whole lot of Victory gardens."

Eddie looked at their baseball field and gulped. "A garden? Here?"

"Why of course," Aunt Daisy replied. "President Roosevelt has asked us to grow as much of our own food as possible. This is our chance to do just that."

"But we don't know anything about growing stuff," Barb said.

"That's the beauty of my idea," Aunt Daisy said. "I do know about growing vegetables. I'm from Oklahoma. We raised a lot of our own food when I was growing up." She walked across the lot, talking as she went. "I was passing by this lot earlier today when I had my inspiration. Then, of course, I thought of you two and what hard workers you are."

Barb smiled at Aunt Daisy and said, "This field could be divided up into lots of little gardens. People could grow what they wanted in their own garden."

"Exactly," Aunt Daisy said and beamed at the twins. In a moment she turned and proceeded across the lot again, talking with every step.

"But what about. . ." Eddie started then stopped. He had been about to ask what about their baseball games. He watched Aunt Daisy and Barb walk on what had been second base. That kind of question might seem downright unpatriotic right now, not to mention a little selfish. Mentally he said good-bye to a summer of baseball games. Besides, this gardening thing might be fun.

In a few days the whole neighborhood buzzed about the Victory garden. Eddie and Barb, together with Carolyn and Warren, spread the word. It seemed there were a lot of people who wanted to do as the president asked. Aunt Daisy said there was no time to spare now that it was April. Gardens should be planted right away to make the most of growing weather.

The following Saturday the vacant lot teemed with gardeners carrying every sort of digging tool. Dad had made a special trip back to their house on Queen Anne Hill that was rented out to another family while the Harringtons ran the hotel. He had rummaged around in the shed until he found an old shovel and hoe and carried them back.

Eddie and Warren had decided to share a small plot, while Barb and Carolyn did the same nearby. They were all excited until Eddie dug into the dirt with the shovel the first time. It only went in a couple of inches. "Must have hit a hard spot," Eddie said to Warren and moved over a few inches to try again. Still the shovel barely bit into the ground. In a few minutes Warren tried his luck, but every inch of the ground was rock hard.

Eddie heard grunts of effort and murmurs of complaint from every part of the lot. Backs unused to digging were soon aching as the gardeners scraped and scratched away at the dirt.

"How in the world will we ever get this ground dug up enough to plant anything?" Barb asked.

Eddie didn't know, so he kept quiet. This gardening was lots harder than Aunt Daisy had made it sound.

A commotion in the street attracted all their attention. Eddie saw a battered old pickup truck pull to the side and park. A homemade-looking trailer was hooked to the back of the truck, but it wasn't the trailer itself that made Eddie look twice. It was the occupants. Two horses stood placidly chewing on wisps of hay, their heads hanging over the high board sides of the trailer. An old gentleman climbed out of the truck and pulled the pegs on the trailer gate.

Eddie's eyes grew round, and he dropped his shovel so he could run to the street with the others close behind. The man was unloading the horses. Aunt Daisy appeared from the other side of the trailer and began giving directions to several men who stood on the sidewalk. They nodded and went to the back of the pickup. Eddie craned his neck but could only see that there was some sort of equipment or machine in the pickup bed. He ran to Aunt Daisy.

"What's going on? What are the horses for?" His questions rolled out.

"You'll see, you'll see," she answered with a big smile. "We're about to garden Oklahoma style."

In fifteen or twenty minutes the horses were harnessed and backed up to the equipment that looked a little like a big butter knife turned sideways.

"What is it?" Barb asked. She stood at Eddie's elbow along with Carolyn and Warren.

"It's a plow," Warren said. "I've seen my uncle use one on his farm."

"Oh, yeah," Eddie said, "now I see. I've never looked at a real one."

"Well, I don't see," Carolyn said. "What does it do?"

"It'll dig up this hard dirt quicker than you can say scat," Warren said.

Sure enough, in a few minutes the old gentleman yelled, "Ye-ho, Tony. Ye-ho, Beauty. Gidyap now." The horses obediently leaned into the harness, and the plow bit into the ground as they pulled it forward. Behind the plow a furrow of brown earth turned over to the sun for the first time in many years.

A cheer rose from the assembled gardeners as they ran to pick up their tools from the lot. The farmer walked beside his horses, guiding them with long reins that trailed along the ground. Another man gripped the handles of the plow and steered as the horses pulled it back and forth across the former baseball field.

Eddie just shook his head and watched. How in the world had Aunt Daisy managed to find a farmer with a plow in the middle of Seattle? It was a couple hours before he got to ask his question. By then the plowing was finished, and Eddie caught up with Aunt Daisy as she helped two older women mark off their sections. "You just have to know the right people," she said in answer to his question and laughed heartily. "Walter, the man with the plow, is my good friend Martha's brother. She goes to my church. That's her over there."

A gray-haired woman wearing a huge hat worked nearby. She had her arms around a small boy, helping him chop at a clod of dirt with a hoe. Her face was wreathed with smiles, and Eddie found himself smiling as well. The April sun was warm on the back of his neck, and a breeze ruffled his hair. The war seemed far away right now.

Eddie and Warren got to work on their small parcel of ground. They hoed and raked until the dirt was smooth. By the middle of the afternoon, they had run out of steam and lay stretched out on the soft bed of earth. Nearby Barb and Carolyn were giving their garden a final raking.

Eddie turned his head a little to sniff the cool dirt. It had a fresh kind of woody smell. The sun was still shining, and he felt like taking a nap right in the middle of the garden.

"Look what I found." A voice accompanied the shadow that passed over Eddie. He shaded his eyes and saw his sister Audrey standing above him. She waved a piece of paper.

"What?" Eddie asked and reluctantly sat up.

"Come over here and look at this," Audrey called to Barb and Carolyn. The two girls dropped their rakes and walked down the narrow path between gardens.

"What have you got, Audrey?" Barb called.

"Let's see," Eddie said and snatched at the paper, but Audrey was too quick for him. She yanked it back and held it high.

"Not so fast," she said. "Everyone gets to look at it." She put the paper at their eye level.

It was a flyer. Eddie read aloud, "Victory Garden Competition. Enter now. Cash prizes for the best sweet corn, tomatoes, beets, carrots, and cucumbers. To be judged by a competent jury on August 9. Sponsored by the South Seattle Neighborhood Association."

"I saw it at the grocery store," Audrey said and passed the flyer to Barb so they could read it again.

In a few moments Barb looked up from reading. Her eyes shone with pleasure. "We can enter. The entry fee is only twenty-five cents. I have that much."

"So do I," Carolyn said.

"So do I," Warren and Eddie said at the same time.

"Let's all enter," Carolyn suggested.

"We can make it boys against the girls," Barb announced with a snap of her fingers. "We'll enter as partners."

"You two in your plot and Warren and I in ours," Eddie said.

"Right," Barb agreed.

Eddie looked at Warren, and matching grins spread across their faces.

"Sounds great to me," Eddie said. "Warren?"

"I'm in," Warren answered.

"Now wait a minute," Audrey said. "You twins better watch out. You've been in trouble before for trying to outdo each other. Why can't you enter the best of both gardens? If you actually manage to grow anything, that is." She gazed pointedly at the bare dirt in front of them, dirt that was a long way from producing prize-winning vegetables.

"It'll be friendly competition. Right, Eddie?" Barb said with a grin.

"Sure, friendly only," Eddie agreed. "It'll just add to the fun if we have our own contest."

"I don't know," Audrey said. She frowned and shook her

head slowly. "You two never seem to be able to have a friendly competition about anything."

"You just wait," Barb said. "This time will be different."

"Different," Eddie echoed. Already his brain was clicking along, thinking how he and Warren could grow the best vegetables. It should be easy to beat the girls, he reasoned. After all, Warren said he helped his uncle on the farm. His friend probably knew all there was to know about gardening. As soon as Audrey walked away, Eddie turned to Barb.

"We're going to beat the socks off you," he said with a knowing nod to his twin.

"Is that so?" Barb said and shook her head. "When did you get to know so much about gardening? I bet we'll leave you standing in that dirt without a single vegetable to enter in the contest."

"That's what you think," Eddie replied, "but you'll be wrong. Because we have a secret weapon, an expert." He picked up his hoe and looked at Warren, who gazed back expectantly.

"And who might that be?" Barb asked.

"Why, Warren here, of course," Eddie said. "He knows tons about gardening. Our cucumbers will be a foot long and our tomatoes almost that wide across." He glanced at Warren. His friend looked astonished.

"We'll be a shoe-in to win prizes and beat you two," Eddie ended with a flourish of his hoe. Meanwhile Warren had stepped closer to Eddie.

"What are you talking about?" Warren hissed in Eddie's ear.

"We'll just see about that," Barb said and stomped off toward the girls' garden followed by Carolyn.

When the girls were safely out of earshot, Eddie turned to

his friend, whose eyebrows were raised high enough to touch his bangs.

"I repeat," Warren said, "what are you talking about? Me! An expert?"

"You said you helped your uncle on his farm," Eddie said. "You know, with the plowing." A mild twinge of concern ran through Eddie. Warren wasn't acting like an expert.

"I said I saw a plow on my uncle's farm," Warren said and ran his hands through his hair. "I was five years old, and my uncle moved to Seattle the next winter. I haven't been on a farm since."

"Oh," Eddie said with a weak grin. "I thought you meant you knew about growing things."

"Don't you think I'd have mentioned that before now?" Warren folded his arms in front of him and frowned at Eddie. "After all, we have been getting ready to plant a garden all week."

Eddie hesitated. "I guess I thought you just didn't want to brag. You mean you don't know about raising tomatoes and carrots and that other stuff?"

"All I know is that I like to eat carrots, and I don't like cucumbers except in pickles."

Eddie leaned on his hoe. This was a definite setback. The girls would be looking for their own secret weapon to beat the boys, especially since Eddie had made such a big deal about Warren. They'd just have to find another way. He wasn't about to let Barb walk off with any prizes for the best vegetables.

CHAPTER 5

Manure Tea

Planting was scheduled for Monday after school, but rain set in Saturday night and continued all day Sunday. Eddie stared out the window at church during the preacher's sermon and out the apartment window that afternoon. The rain fell in a steady stream. It often rained in Seattle, but this was practically a deluge. The gutters along the street ran full, and the bucket his sister Alice put out to catch rainwater to wash her hair over-flowed. Aunt Daisy assured him that it only meant a day or two of delay while the garden dried out, but Eddie didn't want to waste a day of growing time.

Warren came over Sunday afternoon, and the two friends sat on the old sofa in the hotel lobby with Isabel's cat, Mittens, between them and planned their garden. Warren liked to have things written down, so he had a scrap of brown paper and a stubby pencil.

"I think we should grow tomatoes and cucumbers and carrots," Eddie said. "I hate beets."

"And corn gets too tall," Warren said as he wrote down their choices.

"We'll have three chances to win the prizes and beat the girls," Eddie said.

"Speaking of beating the girls," Warren said, "have you had any more bright ideas about how we're actually going to get this stuff to grow?" He reached over to pick up a packet of seed he had brought with him from home. "The instructions on the back of this package don't say too much."

Eddie took the seed packet and read the back for a minute before looking up with a frown. "I see what you mean. But don't you think that you just put the seeds in the ground, cover them up with dirt, and they grow?" All the times he had seen Mr. Lazarini working with his pots of plants, it had seemed so easy. And Mr. Lazarini had beautiful, healthy-looking flowers and herbs.

"I think it's harder than that," Warren said.

Eddie stared at the lobby floor and thought. "There must be someone who can help us. I already thought of Aunt Daisy, but she said she wasn't getting in the middle of another contest."

The boys fell silent as they racked their brains for a solution.

"Hi, there," a cheerful voice called, rousing Eddie out of his thoughts. It was Mr. Lazarini. "You two look mighty thoughtful there. You working on a big problem?" The neighbor had a sackful of groceries in his arms.

Eddie looked at his Italian friend for a moment and then turned slowly to Warren. He could tell by Warren's expression that he was having the same idea. Eddie jumped up from the couch, accidentally dumping Mittens to the floor, and went over to Mr. Lazarini. "Let me carry those for you."

"That's not necessary, son," Mr. Lazarini said, "but thanks for offering."

"I insist," Eddie said, "because we want to talk to you about that problem we've been thinking over." Eddie succeeded in taking the groceries and motioned for Warren to come.

Mr. Lazarini grinned and led the way to his apartment. "Now just what trouble have you boys got yourself into this time?" He opened his front door and let Eddie and Warren go in first.

"Not exactly trouble this time," Eddie said, "but we do need some help."

"Let's see what I can do then." Mr. Lazarini closed his door behind them.

It was the next day at recess before Eddie and Warren got to talk over Mr. Lazarini's advice. It had been time for supper last night when they left the neighbor's apartment, and Warren had to hurry home. The rain had finally stopped, so the boys met on the playground to talk.

"What did you think about his growing tips?" Warren asked.

"It didn't sound too hard," Eddie said. "In fact he made it sound downright easy." If you had the right fertilizer, that is.

Mr. Lazarini called it manure tea, and it sounded nasty, but if that was what it took to grow prize-winning vegetables, then that's what they'd use.

"When are we getting the manure?" Warren asked.

"I suppose this afternoon after school is as good a time as any since we can't plant until the ground dries out some," Eddie said.

Mr. Lazarini had told them about a delivery service that had to go back to using horses and wagons for deliveries after their old truck broke down. He said they would have plenty of manure to get rid of.

"Too bad we weren't looking for manure on Saturday morning when the plow horses came to town," Warren said. "They left plenty of droppings behind that the farmer had to clean up."

Eddie laughed and nodded. "Meet me at the corner at the cigar shop at four o'clock this afternoon."

Warren saluted, and they both ran for the school door because the bell was clanging.

By the time the boys met, the sun had chased the lingering clouds out of the sky. "This should dry out the garden pretty quick," Eddie said as they fell into step together.

"How will we carry the manure?" Warren asked.

Eddie whipped a faded cotton sack out of his back pocket. "Mama said we could have this old flour sack."

"Did she know what we were putting in it?"

"She didn't ask," Eddie answered, "but she didn't mention wanting it back."

The delivery service's makeshift stable was close to the waterfront. The boys loved that part of Seattle because there was always so much to see. Frank had promised to take them sometime to see the underground tunnels that snaked beneath the streets near the waterfront. The tunnels were left over from the last century before the street level had been raised.

But this time, the boys went directly to the delivery service office and asked the woman sitting at a desk if they could collect some manure. She laughed and said she imagined that would be just fine.

"So what do we pick it up with?" Warren asked a few minutes later when they stood in the entry to the horse stalls and stared at the straw on the ground. A good supply of manure was scattered there. Luckily the horses were out on a delivery.

Eddie looked around. "Good question. Why don't you just use your fingers?"

"No, sir!" Warren said loudly. "I'm not touching that stuff with my bare hands."

Eddie grinned. "I didn't think so." He looked around again and saw a broken piece of board in the corner. He leaned over and picked it up. "Use this." He held it out to Warren.

"Go ahead," Warren said and took a step back.

Eddie grinned and squatted down next to a likely looking pile of manure. "Get the bag," he ordered.

Warren jerked the flour bag out of Eddie's back pocket and held it open.

Carefully Eddie scooped up a small ball of manure and transferred it to the bag. He repeated his actions several times.

"That stuff smells terrible," Warren said and turned his head as far to one side as possible while still holding the bag open.

"It is a little ripe," Eddie agreed. At last he threw his makeshift scoop back into the corner and stood up. "There, we're done. That should make gallons of manure tea."

Warren stood, holding the bag as far in front of him as possible.

"Are you going to carry it home that way?" Eddie asked. "You look pretty silly."

"I guess so, because I'm not getting any closer than this to that stuff," Warren replied.

"Here, give it to me," Eddie said and took the bag. He held it by the top and kept the contents well away from his legs as he walked. In this way the two gardeners began the trip home.

They had only gone a block or two when Warren jabbed Eddie in the side.

"What's that for?" Eddie protested as he shifted his smelly burden.

"Quiet," Warren ordered. "Look over there." He pointed to a group of men clustered in front of a tavern the boys were passing.

Eddie stared at the men who laughed as they smoked and talked. What was he supposed to see? His puzzlement ended when he recognized a chubby fellow. It was Sal.

Eddie gave Warren a look and they hurried on down the street to a doorway that they stepped into. They peeked back at the men, careful to stay out of sight.

"I thought he was on the day shift now," Warren said.

"Mr. Lazarini said yesterday that he was on twelve-hour day shifts."

"Not today," Warren said. "Do you think he's skipping work?"

"Maybe," Eddie said. "Isabel's always complaining about how many people don't show up for work every day at the factory. She says it slows the whole factory down. I guess the shipyard is probably the same."

"And this is Sal we're talking about," Warren said and peeked back again. "Say, look at his hands."

Eddie looked again. Sal was tipping the ash off the end of his cigarette. His hand looked red. "What is that?"

"Paint, maybe?" Warren ventured.

"It doesn't really look like paint." While Eddie watched, Sal threw his cigarette into the street and went inside the tavern with the other men. "I don't know what that guy is up to. I wonder why he's lying to Mr. Lazarini?"

"Should we tell Mr. Lazarini that we saw Sal?" Warren asked.

Eddie frowned as they started down the street again. "No, I don't think so. He sets such store by family. It might make him feel bad to know that Sal wasn't at work." Eddie wished he could find out more about Sal. Mr. Lazarini was too nice a man to have a lying cousin hanging around.

It was getting late by the time Eddie and Warren reached the alley behind the hotel with their smelly bag.

"What will we put the manure tea in?" Warren asked.

"An old bucket should work," Eddie said. "I forgot to ask if we should put it on once when we plant the seeds or more often than that."

"I don't want to have to go back and collect more manure," Warren said firmly, "so save some of it for later. Put it under that broken crate over there. I'll find a bucket for the tea." Warren looked around. "It's getting dark. We better get this finished."

Eddie moved the crate aside a little. "There's an old bucket down by the fire escape stairs. Go get it while I dump some of this manure. We'll get water and mix up the whole mess." He held the bag out and dumped part of its contents on the ground under the wooden crate.

Warren returned in a few minutes with a bucket. "Here, this should do it." He handed the bucket to Eddie. "It even had water in it already."

"Good," Eddie said and took the bucket. "Mr. Lazarini said to put the manure in a bag into the water." Eddie knotted the top of the flour bag and gingerly poked it in the bucket. It floated until he took a stick and shoved it farther into the bucket.

"I don't see how this will make the vegetables grow," Warren confessed.

"Mr. Lazarini said it was like steak and spinach to plants," Eddie said and poked at the sack some more.

"I have to go home," Warren said. "Do you leave the sack in the water?"

"Hmm, I don't know," Eddie said. "I'll have to ask Mr. Lazarini that, too."

"You better take it out for now," Warren said, "until you can ask him. It might be too strong if you leave it in there until tomorrow."

"You're right," Eddie agreed. "We wouldn't want to kill our seeds before they even get started." He used the stick to lift out the sopping sack that was now an unfortunate shade of brown and scooted it under the crate with the extra manure. The bucket of freshly brewed manure tea was left beside the back hotel door. He'd check with Mr. Lazarini later to see if he should put the sack back in the water.

Supper was Eddie's wartime favorite—beans and corn-bread. He ate until he was stuffed and then sat down to listen to the war news on the radio. Sometimes it seemed like that was all that was on the radio these days, but he knew it was important to know what was happening all those thousands of miles away on the other side of the world. The family gathered around the radio to listen together most evenings.

Except for Alice, that is. His older sister often skipped that ritual. She said it was almost as hard not to hear any news related to her fiancé, Jim, as it was to hear bad news. Jim Watson had been missing in action in the Philippines for two years.

Eddie noticed Alice walk past the living-room door in their apartment, carrying a bucket. He didn't pay much attention since she was always washing her hair with the rainwater she collected.

The announcer had just signed off when a scream echoed through the apartment. Eddie jumped up, followed by everyone else. The scream had come from the bathroom, and now there were angry noises coming from the same room.

In seconds they all crowded in the open bathroom door. A red-faced Alice with fire in her eyes stood before them. She was dressed in her bathrobe, and her hair dripped water over her face and robe.

"What's wrong?" Mama asked.

"I started to wash my hair." Alice waved at the sink. "With my rainwater. The same rainwater that I always collect. In the same bucket." She glared at her family. "But it seems that someone has put some horrible concoction in my bucket without telling me." She held out a strand of her hair. "It smells like. . . like." She hesitated as words apparently failed her. "It smells like a barnyard," she burst out finally.

Eddie backed away from the group. This was as good a

time as any to visit Mr. Lazarini.

"Eddie!" Mama grabbed his arm.

"Yes," he answered and smiled as innocently as he could.

"Do you know anything about this little mishap?"

"Sort of," he managed to squeak out. "Warren and I were making manure tea for fertilizer for our garden."

"Manure tea!" Alice shrieked. "I put manure on my hair. Let me at him."

Eddie wiggled behind Frank, who was laughing uproariously. Alice tried to grab her little brother, and in the process the foul-smelling water in her hair flew in droplets over all of them.

"Wait, wait, Alice," Mama said and glared at Dad, who looked to be holding in laughter, too. "We'll take care of Eddie. You wash your hair."

Eddie peeked out from behind Frank. "It's good for plants. Maybe it would be good for your hair, too."

Alice made one more lunge at Eddie before she allowed Audrey to lead her back into the bathroom.

"I'm waiting," Mother said, tapping her foot as she waited for him to go into the living room. "This better be good."

Eddie grinned again. "Oh, it is. It's patriotic, even." He hoped that fertilizer for a Victory garden fell into that area.

Mama just rolled her eyes and shoved him in the living room.

CHAPTER 6

Victory Garden Contest

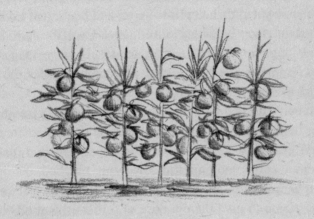

"Too bad Mama made you share your *secret weapon*," Barb said one hot July day when the twins arrived at the Victory garden to work in their plots.

"If you've said that once, you've said it a hundred times," Eddie said as he chopped out a weed that dared to grow near the tomatoes.

"Without that manure tea, our vegetables probably wouldn't be nearly as big as yours," Barb said and wrinkled her nose at her brother. "You might have won the contest hands down. Too

55

bad that won't happen now." She wiped a pretend tear from the corner of her eye and walked off.

Barb had been teasing him about the manure tea for weeks now. Alice had forgiven him long ago, but Barb wouldn't let him forget it. According to Mama, it wasn't important who had the biggest tomatoes or cucumbers. It was important to do everything possible to help win the war so Steve and Jim and all the soldiers could come home. Apparently Barb didn't agree.

Both gardens now had large glossy tomatoes and long shiny cucumbers. The girls had planted corn and beets, and Eddie had to admit that the vegetables looked great. Even the carrots were fat and long. Some of the other gardens had vegetables that looked almost as good, but Eddie was convinced that the fertilizer had made the difference.

Actually he had one more of Mr. Lazarini's growing tips that he had been using. It was more secret than the manure tea. Even Warren didn't know, but Eddie hoped it would make the difference come judging time. Hoeing finished, he looked around to see if anyone was near before he sat down among the tomato plants to give them a dose of fertilizer. But this time it wasn't manure tea.

"Sam, you're looking especially fine today," Eddie said in a low voice. "And Oscar, I've never seen you looking so healthy. Mary, your tomatoes have grown since yesterday. Now, all of you just hold on a day or two. Dad says it's bound to rain tomorrow."

A chuckle made Eddie jerk his head up. Warren stood over him with a puzzled grin on his face.

"What are you doing?" Warren asked. "Talking to the tomato plants?"

Eddie jumped up and dusted off the seat of his pants. "Quiet!" he ordered before glancing around to see if Barb was still in her own plot. "It's my other secret weapon. Mr. Lazarini says that he always talks to his plants. He thinks that makes them grow better."

"So you *were* talking to them," Warren said.

Eddie tilted his head and grinned before nodding. "I gave them names so it wouldn't feel quite so silly. This is Mary and Sam and Oscar, and the others have names, too."

Warren looked uncertain whether he should laugh or not. Finally he shrugged and asked, "Do you think it's working?"

"I can't be sure," Eddie said, "but I think so. Some of our tomatoes seem to be growing faster than the girls' tomatoes. Mr. Lazarini says it works for him. What can it hurt? If you don't tell anyone, that is."

"Oh, I won't be telling anyone that my best friend is sitting in the middle of a tomato patch telling the plants how wonderful they are," Warren said. He plopped down in the dirt near the cucumbers. "I'm ready. What do cucumbers need to hear to make them grow?"

Eddie laughed and sat down by Warren. "I usually tell them how shiny and green they're looking, but you don't have to talk to them today. It's not really their turn."

"Whew!" Warren said. "Thank goodness. I may have to think a little about what to say, especially to the carrots. They're probably more particular than cucumbers. Thank goodness we don't have any sweet corn."

The boys flopped backward in the dirt and laughed.

"What's so funny?" Barb called and walked down the path to stand over them.

"Oh, nothing," Eddie assured her. He wasn't about to give away another gardening secret to his sister. Warren got up and went with Barb to see the girls' vegetables, but Eddie remained where he was. He liked the smell of nearly ripe tomatoes that blended with the aroma of warm dirt.

The Victory garden had helped him not think about the war so much, which was funny since the only reason they had a Victory garden was because of the war. It felt good to hear his parents talk about normal, everyday things like how long before the tomatoes would be ripe, and he liked to argue with his brothers and sisters about the best kind of pickles to make with the cucumbers.

A bundle of letters from Steve had finally arrived in May and twice more since then. He was safe so far, but there were new worries. Just last week the papers had headlined the news that the Allies had invaded Italy. The family couldn't be sure, but it seemed likely that Steve's unit had been part of that action. Eddie rolled on his side and watched as a ladybug crawled up one of Oscar's stems. Eddie prayed for his brother every day, but sometimes he wondered how God handled this war business. What if the Italian and German families were praying for their soldiers to defeat the Americans at the same time that the Americans were praying the opposite. What would God do?

He was finding out that war was more complicated than the good guys against the bad guys like in Roy Rogers movies. The family had received a letter yesterday from the Wakamutsus. They were still in the internment camp in Idaho. Eddie hadn't known the Japanese family very well, but he knew they were loyal Americans. It was hard to understand why they should be locked up.

Mr. Lazarini's brother, Antonio, still lived in Italy, and Eddie could see that his Italian neighbor was very worried about his brother. If Antonio was half as nice as his younger brother was, Eddie knew that he wasn't one of the bad guys. God had his work cut out for him trying to sort out this war mess.

Eddie sat up. It was time to go home and do some chores. He glanced around but saw no sign of Barb. He leaned over and whispered another encouraging word to Oscar. What could it hurt?

At last August arrived and with it the day of the contest. Eddie and Barb met Warren and Carolyn at the Victory garden early that morning. Aunt Daisy had said it would be best to pick everything at the last minute to preserve the freshest taste possible.

Eddie held up a just-picked tomato and yelled across the garden to Barb, "This one looks like it would taste delicious. It's awfully plump and firm, and would you look at that color?"

"I've got one here that's twice as big, and talk about color," Barb yelled back, "why it's perfect. And I can tell from the smell that it's going to knock those judges' socks off."

"Why do you two argue all the time?" Warren asked.

Eddie looked up from picking another tomato. "I don't know," he admitted. "We didn't used to, but now we just do. She always has to be best at everything." Eddie didn't say anything else. It was true. He and Barb argued a lot more nowadays. He wasn't sure he liked it, but that's the way it was.

At last they all finished picking a good amount of each of their ripe vegetables. They took them to Eddie and Barb's apartment to wash and choose which ones to put on plates for the judging.

Barb was hovering over the kitchen sink, lovingly washing each carrot and ear of corn. Eddie stood nearby, waiting for his turn to use the sink.

"You don't have to take each bit of corn silk off by itself," he burst out, unable to wait any longer. He kept looking at the clock. If Barb didn't hurry up, they were going to be late to the contest.

"Oh, don't be such a grouch," she said and took another ear from Carolyn who stood nearby. "We want them to be perfectly clean for the judges." With exaggerated care she peered at the ear of corn and plucked nearly invisible strands of corn silk from it. Or at least they looked invisible to Eddie.

"I mean it, Barb, hurry up." It took a lot to make Eddie angry, but his sister was getting near his limits.

"Eddie, go away and leave us alone. Go to the sink in the laundry room or use the bathroom sink." Barb continued to pluck at the corn silk. "We still have to wash our tomatoes."

"The bathroom sink is too small, and we don't have time to traipse over to the laundry room." Eddie's frustration was mounting. "Hurry up!" His words came out loud. Probably louder than he intended. Carolyn jumped when he yelled and bumped her arm on the girls' tomato basket, which had been resting precariously on the edge of the counter.

The next thing Eddie knew, the tomatoes were spilling out of the basket as it tumbled to the floor. He grabbed for them, but it was too late. They hit the floor with a splat as some of them split and spattered juice and seeds everywhere.

"Eddie Harrington," Barb roared, "you did that on purpose."

"No, I didn't," Eddie yelled. "I'm sorry. It was an accident." He got down on the floor to pick up the squishy tomatoes.

"You just want to make sure that you win the contest."

Barb's face was red.

"That's not true. It was an accident," Eddie repeated. "I didn't touch that basket."

"You didn't have to."

"You shouldn't have left it sitting on the edge. It's your fault."

"What's going on here?" A calm voice asked from the kitchen door.

It was Mama, and Eddie knew that tone. It was calm all right, dangerously calm.

It didn't take long for Mama to sort things out. In a few minutes the law had been laid down. The twins were forbidden to enter the contest. If Carolyn and Warren wanted to take the vegetables and enter, they could.

"I don't want to hear that kind of ugly talk between my twins ever again," Mama said. "If we don't all work together while this terrible war rages, we will not survive. God expects us to love each other and show that love in every way."

Mama walked off down the hall, her heels clicking briskly on the linoleum floor. Eddie and Barb looked at each other.

"I'm sorry," Eddie said after a moment.

"Me, too," Barb said.

Eddie plopped down on a kitchen chair. "Now we can't enter the contest."

"I guess it's just as well," Barb said. "Our tomatoes are ruined."

"Your corn is fine," Eddie pointed out, "and terribly clean, too."

Barb grinned at Eddie. "It sure is."

Carolyn and Warren had been conferring while Eddie and

Barb talked and now turned to the twins with big smiles.

"We have an idea," Carolyn said.

"A great idea, in fact," Warren added.

"Warren and I will enter the vegetables like your mother said. But we'll just enter tomatoes and cucumbers for the boys and carrots and sweet corn for the girls," Carolyn said. "That way we might win, but we won't be competing against each other."

"If we had thought of that to start with," Eddie said, "we wouldn't be in so much trouble. Come on. Let's leave, or we're going to miss the whole thing."

The hall was packed with people. Many had entered their prize vegetables, but just as many seemed to have come for the fun of it. It wasn't an ordinary thing to have a vegetable-growing contest in the middle of a big city like Seattle, but then nothing was ordinary during the war.

Eddie sniffed with pleasure as they entered the big basement room. The fresh smells of all the produce blended together to make an aroma that was almost like vegetable soup. Soon the long tables were covered with plates of corn and beets and tomatoes. Cucumbers and carrots sat alongside.

With much laughter and pretend ceremony, the judges entered the hall. There were two men and two women, and Eddie thought he saw their eyes widen when they saw all the entries. They didn't say anything but gamely began to work their way down the tables, looking and sniffing and sometimes tasting.

The hall was hot, and after awhile Eddie and Warren went to find a drinking fountain. They took turns taking long slurps from the fountain in the hall entryway. While Eddie waited for Warren to take one more drink, he glanced out the open door.

On the sidewalk stood Sal talking to a short brown-haired man who didn't look a thing like anyone Eddie had ever seen in the neighborhood. In spite of the hot day, the man was dressed in a black suit complete with a necktie and shiny black shoes. Eddie hadn't seen any shoes that new looking since the war started.

"Look out there," Eddie said in a low voice to Warren and pointed.

Warren looked and groaned. "Sal has more unexpected days off from work than anyone I've ever seen. Too bad our fathers can't get off as often."

The pair outside moved to one side so the boys couldn't see them anymore. "Let's see what they're doing," Eddie suggested. Before Warren could respond, he walked the few steps to the door.

Sal and his dressed-up friend were walking across the street toward a drugstore.

"Come on, let's follow them," Eddie said.

"Should we do that?" Warren asked and hesitated in the doorway.

Eddie chewed his lip for a moment. He knew what his mother would say about snooping, but this was a special circumstance. He was almost sure of that. "That guy Sal's with looks pretty suspicious. You said yourself that Sal is always off work. We better check them out."

Warren nodded and they ran across the street to peer in the drugstore window. Sal and the other man were just sitting down in a booth near the back.

"Come on," Eddie said. "We can pretend to look at the comic books on that rack."

Warren looked a little alarmed but followed Eddie behind a counter and back to the magazine rack, which was only a few feet from the booth where Sal and the man sat. Eddie picked up a comic book and held it right in front of his face. Warren did likewise. They were careful to keep their backs to the two men.

"Everything is coming along just as planned," Sal said.

"You seem to have the knack for it," the other man said.

A small hand tugged on Eddie's elbow. "I want that comic book."

Eddie ducked his head enough to see that a small boy stood beside him.

"Go away," Eddie said in a low voice. This was no time to attract attention.

"I want that one," the boy repeated loudly and grabbed for the comic book that Eddie held in front of his face. It slipped, and Eddie ducked down as the boy pulled the comic book away. All Eddie could think of was to get out of sight, so he crawled behind the nearby cigarette counter and on toward the front of the drugstore. He looked back and saw that Warren had followed.

At the end of the counter they jumped up and dashed out the door. They ran across the street and didn't stop until they were inside the hall once more.

"Do you think they saw us?" Warren asked.

"I don't think so, but that kid sure messed things up," Eddie said disgustedly. "It was just starting to get good."

"What do you suppose is coming along as planned?" Warren asked.

"I don't know," Eddie said, "but I wish I could figure it out."

"Eddie, Warren, there you are," Barb said as she rushed

up. "Come on. The judges are finished. Let's see if we won a ribbon."

Eddie cast one last glance across the street before hurrying after the girls and Warren. Checking up on Sal would have to wait a while longer.

There on the table in the hall sat a red second place ribbon on the boys' tomatoes and a red ribbon on the girls' sweet corn as well.

"Not bad for beginners," Alice said when she walked up behind them to join in the admiration.

"Our tomatoes probably would have won. . ." Barb started to say but stopped.

Eddie looked at his sister. "What did you say?"

"Never mind," she said with a grin. "We did great."

Eddie grinned back. It was the first time in weeks that he didn't feel like arguing with his twin. This time she made sense.

CHAPTER 7

Goats and Floats

Eddie sniffed as he slammed the front apartment door after school one afternoon in September. The smell of hot tomatoes filled the air.

"Don't slam the door!" His mom's voice came from the kitchen.

"Sorry," he yelled as he tossed his arithmetic book at a

nearby chair and ran across the living room to the kitchen door.

"Slow down," Mama ordered from where she stood over a steaming pot at the stove. Her forehead glistened with sweat, and she pushed back a strand of hair that had fallen across her face.

"Yes, ma'am," Eddie said and flopped in a chair at the kitchen table where a row of glass jars sat. Alice stood at the table cutting up a big pile of tomatoes one after another.

"What are you doing?" Eddie asked.

Alice gave him a withering look. "What does it look like we're doing? What are we doing every day? Canning these infernal tomatoes, that's what."

"I'm getting downright sick of the smell of tomatoes. Why do you keep canning them?" Eddie asked, more to tease his sister than because he wanted an answer.

"You'll be glad enough to have these canned tomatoes, come winter," Mama said tartly. "The food shortages make it harder all the time to find the things we like, and these vegetables will taste pretty good in January."

Eddie looked over at the wooden shelves that Dad had put up in the corner of the crowded kitchen. Jars of bright yellow corn, orange carrots, deep red tomatoes, and purple beets were lined up there. He could smell the pickles that Mama was making in a big stone crock near the table. The tomatoes Alice was slicing would soon be joining the others. It seemed like his mom and older sisters had been canning for weeks.

"Our gardens did good," Eddie said with satisfaction.

"Almost too good," Alice said.

Eddie grinned. The Victory gardens had produced bushels of vegetables. The corn and beets and carrots were done now, but the cucumbers and tomatoes kept coming. Everyone in the hotel had been well supplied with vegetables. Eddie had taken some tomatoes to Mr. Lazarini just yesterday. With Sal to feed, Mr. Lazarini needed all the help he could get.

Eddie had kept a close eye on Sal since the contest but hadn't found out a single new thing about the plans that the two men had mentioned in the drugstore. But he wasn't giving up. Any little bit of information might be a clue, so Eddie was staying alert.

"Why are you so late?" Mama asked. "Audrey took over in the office an hour ago. And where is Barb?" She opened the refrigerator and poured a glass of milk that she placed in front of Eddie with a big slice of bread.

"Thanks," Eddie replied. "She's talking to Carolyn. I had an emergency Scout meeting after school."

"Emergency?" Mama questioned.

"Well, not exactly emergency," Eddie admitted. "We wanted to start planning our float for the parade. We think the Girl Scouts are doing a float, too." He took a big bite of bread and followed it with a gulp of milk.

"What parade is that?" Alice asked.

"The parade for the third war loan drive." Eddie shook his head at his sister's ignorance. There had already been two war loan drives, and he was looking forward to this one. For the other drives there had been rallies and parades and lots of excitement, and this one promised to be the same.

"I see," Alice said. "So you're making a float."

"It's going to be a humdinger," Eddie said before popping the last of his bread into his mouth.

"No doubt the Girl Scout float will be a humdinger, too," Alice said.

"Not as good as ours," Eddie insisted.

"I don't want to hear that kind of talk," Mama said. She lowered one more canning jar into the kettle of hot water before turning to her youngest son. "It's fine to build a float, but it's not fine to spend all your time trying to outdo someone else. The purpose of the parade is to convince people to buy war bonds and stamps, not to dazzle them with a float."

"I know," Eddie said, "but the girls—"

"No buts about it," Mama said firmly. "Before long, you and Warren will be wanting to impress those girls instead of show them up."

"Not us," Eddie said with a decisive shake of his head. He couldn't imagine wanting to impress a girl. He liked Carolyn fine, and Barb was a lot of fun when she wasn't trying to beat him at something, but he didn't care a thing about impressing either one of them.

The apartment front door burst open and then banged shut.

"Don't slam the door!" Mama hollered. The words were barely out of her mouth when Barb propelled herself into the kitchen.

"You won't believe how spectacular the Girl Scout float will be," she announced to everyone before dropping into a chair beside Eddie.

"You're right," Eddie said, "I won't believe it."

"Eddie." His mother's voice held a warning.

He grinned and passed Barb the piece of bread that Mama had handed him. "So what will your float look like?"

"I can't tell you," Barb said. "It's a secret, but it'll be better than what you boys make. That's for sure."

"Barb," Mama said sharply, "I've just been all through this

with your brother. No more competition. Work together for a change."

"But Mama," Barb said, "we can't do that. The Girl Scouts want their own float."

"And so do the Boy Scouts," Eddie added.

"Well, fine, but I don't want any arguing, or you two will be sitting out the parade just like the Victory garden contest. Understand?" Mama stared at the twins until Eddie nodded and saw Barb do the same.

"Speaking of Victory gardens," Alice said. "I just cut up the last tomato. Hallelujah!"

Eddie went off to do his chores, but he thought the whole time about the parade. Maybe they couldn't have an official contest, but at least the Boy Scouts could make the best float possible. They needed a good idea, and that wasn't all. A float was usually on a wagon pulled by a tractor or truck. What with gas and tire rationing, there weren't many vehicles left to be used for floats. This was going to take some thought.

Eddie couldn't wait to get to school so the boys could huddle together and plan their float. Most of the boys in his class were in Boy Scouts, and the others liked to give their opinions. School was especially fun this year anyway. Carolyn and Warren were in the same class with Barb and Eddie, which hadn't happened last year, and to make it even better, they had the same teacher as Barb and Eddie had had last year. Mrs. Potter had changed from third grade to fourth grade. She was young and pretty and thought learning should be fun. Eddie was sure that he had the best teacher in the world.

Mrs. Potter gave her class some time almost every day to work on projects related to the war effort. She said their work was just as important as what adults did and that the soldiers said so, too. Eddie thought Mrs. Potter should know since her husband Donald was a pilot in the army air corps. Mr. Potter's picture sat on Mrs. Potter's desk next to her pencil cup. Last year he wrote two letters to their class, and his wife talked about him often.

Mrs. Potter had tacked up a big map of the world on one wall of their classroom, and the students had pinned tiny American flags on every place where soldiers they knew served. For a few, the flags represented their fathers, and for others it was brothers or sisters or other relatives. Barb and Eddie had carefully pinned up Steve's flag in Italy and one for Jim Watson in the Philippines.

Some students pinned up little black crosses on the map for soldiers they knew who had died. Carolyn put a cross over Hawaii because her brother had died in the attack on Pearl Harbor. Mrs. Potter said it was good to remember those who died, that it helped the pain go away just a little. Eddie was thankful that there were many more flags than crosses on the map. That gave him hope that Steve's flag wouldn't have to be changed to a cross.

A week passed, and Eddie was getting worried about the Boy Scouts' float. Every idea they'd had so far didn't work out. One of the troop members, Freddie, had thought he could borrow a farm wagon from his uncle who lived south of Seattle. His uncle said that was fine, but unless Freddie wanted to pull it himself, there was no way to get it into Seattle. His uncle's old truck had long since been parked because the tires were shot and new ones were hard to get. The uncle's family rode the bus everywhere.

"I don't see how we can make a float," Warren said, one afternoon after school, "when we don't have anything to put it on." He and Eddie were collecting fat in the hotel again.

"True," Eddie agreed, "but that's not all. If we had a wagon, how would we decorate it? I haven't been able to find any paper that we can use for streamers. All I have is two old posters from the Victory garden contest. We could write on the back of those."

"This war and all the shortages mess up everything," Warren said.

Eddie nodded. He couldn't argue with Warren's words. There were exciting things about the war, but mostly it was a lot of trouble and pretty scary.

The friends made a couple more stops to get fat and headed for Mr. Lazarini's apartment. "Have the girls come up with anything?" Warren asked.

"I'm not sure," Eddie answered, "but I think so. Barb and Carolyn were making a list last night, and all the girls were giggling and talking at recess today."

"They've thought of something," Warren said glumly, "that's for sure."

"Don't give up," Eddie said. "We'll figure it out. Those girls aren't going to beat us." At least he hoped not. He was pretty sure that he had heard Barb tell Mama that Esther Stratton's brother had agreed to use his motorcycle to pull an old trailer that Carolyn's father knew about. If that were so, then they were halfway to having a real float. It would be small, but small or large didn't matter if you didn't have anything at all to pull like the Boy Scouts.

"Hi there, boys," Mr. Lazarini said and ushered the boys into his apartment. "I'm just getting the dirty clothes ready to take to the Chinese laundry." He inspected a blue shirt he held. "I don't know where in the world Sal gets these nasty red stains on his work shirts."

"Maybe at work?" Eddie asked with a grin. He took his larger can over to the stove where he knew Mr. Lazarini's small fat-collecting can sat.

Mr. Lazarini chuckled. "Seems likely, doesn't it? Only problem is that Sal is a welder. He's said before that he wears a heavy leather apron. These stains aren't burns anyhow. They're more like ink." The older man peered again at the shirt in his hand. "Oh, well. It doesn't matter. Stains are stains, and these don't come out." He dropped the shirt in a pile of clothes. "What are you two up to these days?"

Eddie motioned for Warren to steady the big can while he poured the contents of the smaller one into it. "We're trying to make a float for the parade Saturday, but so far we don't have a wagon or anything to put on it."

"And we don't have a good idea, either," Warren added. "We think the Girl Scouts do, though."

"Always trying to beat the girls, aren't you?" Mr. Lazarini asked.

"Not much chance of that this time," Warren said.

"We'll think of something," Eddie said and took the big can from Warren once more. "Any ideas, Mr. Lazarini?"

"Let's see," Mr. Lazarini said and frowned in thought. "Hmm, an idea for a float, you say."

"Anything at all," Eddie said.

"I wonder if you might not look at the problem from a different direction," the old man said. "Perhaps a float isn't the only possibility—or at least not the wagon or trailer kind of float."

"Like what?" Eddie asked.

"I saw something in a magazine the other day," Mr. Lazarini said. "Now where did I put that?" He leaned over to rummage in a box that sat by his big chair. In a moment he pulled a magazine out and flipped it open. "Here it is," he said and pointed to a picture. "I thought this was a great idea for a slogan."

Eddie put the fat can down and crowded close with Warren to stare at the magazine. He saw a picture of several boys with one wearing a Boy Scout uniform. It looked like they were in a parade because they were lined up in a street and carried a big banner. Eddie stared at the banner. It said, THE AXIS CAN'T GET OUR GOAT. BUY MORE WAR BONDS AND STAMPS. In the midst of the boys stood a goat.

"Wow!" Eddie said. "This is great. We wouldn't need a wagon or anything."

"We'd just dress in our Scout uniforms, kind of like we were soldiers," Warren said.

"And we could make a big sign with those old posters," Eddie added.

"But where would we find a goat?" Warren asked and looked glum once more.

Eddie's smile broadened. "I think we can take care of that, too. Remember how Allen Lutchesky talks about having to drink goat's milk and sometimes he brings goat cheese to school?"

"He hates it," Warren said with a nod.

"His grandmother lives farther south, where she has a little backyard. She keeps a goat in it. We'll borrow her goat for the parade." Eddie went to the door. "Come on, let's go call Allen. Thanks, Mr. Lazarini."

"Thanks a bunch," Warren added and followed Eddie.

"You're welcome, boys," Mr. Lazarini said. "It was nothing."

The boys were in the hall before Mr. Lazarini called, "Wait, don't forget your can."

Eddie darted back to pick up the can he had left in the middle of Mr. Lazarini's floor. "Sorry about that," he said. "Guess I'm kind of excited. The girls sure won't have a goat."

"Probably not," Mr. Lazarini conceded with a smile and shut his door.

"Let's go to the hotel office and call Allen," Eddie said. He hurried down the hall. "I think this will be great."

Eddie was relieved that the goat idea seemed to work out fine. Allen's grandmother said she didn't care if Maizie came to town for the big parade. They made the sign, found a fake mustache for Aaron Smithson, who was to be Hitler pretending to get their goat, and waited for Friday.

The parade was scheduled for 2:00 P.M., and school was to be let out early for the event. Mrs. Potter had a hard time settling the fourth grade down to take their spelling test that morning.

The Girl Scouts had brought their float to the school playground early on Friday since the parade starting point was nearby. Eddie had to admit that their float was nice. They had used all sorts of tin cans and other scrap to build a shape that looked quite a bit like a tank. When the parade was over, they would haul the float straight to the collection station for recycling.

Everyone who could hurried home at lunchtime to put on costumes or bring other items for the parade. The boys all met in a corner of the playground right before time for the bell to be sure they had everything.

"Hey, guys," a breathless voice yelled. Eddie turned to see Allen pulling at a rope attached to a brown and white goat who didn't seem too excited about being led across the playground. The animal stopped every few feet and planted her feet until Allen tugged and held out a piece of grass. Then the goat would walk another few steps, stop, and repeat the process.

Eddie and Warren and the others ran up to Allen and the goat. "I thought your sister was going to bring Maizie right before the parade," Eddie said.

"She got called in to work," Allen said, "and my mother said she wasn't touching this ornery goat. Since my uncle brought Maizie from Grandma's this morning, she's already chewed up one side of my mother's clothes basket and the corner of a sheet." Allen raised his hands in defeat. "I had to bring her with me."

"We'll tie her up to the fence in the shade over there," Eddie said and pointed across the graveled playground to near where the Girl Scout float was parked, waiting for the parade. "Quick, before the bell rings, run and pull her some grass to eat."

Warren and a couple other boys ran toward the front of the school where there was a patch of grass.

"Come on, Maizie," Eddie coaxed. "Let's go." He put his hands by Allen's on the rope and tugged gently. After giving a delicate snort, Maizie allowed herself to be led over to the fence, where the boys tied her rope in a double knot. In a minute Warren and the others were back with handfuls of grass, which she immediately began munching.

"I hope she'll stay put," Allen said nervously. The bell rang, and the boys rushed to line up at the back door of the school.

"She'll be fine," Eddie assured him. "She's tied up and has grass to eat. Besides, we'll be dismissed in less than an hour."

Allen cast a last worried glance at his goat as they marched into school. "I hope so."

Mrs. Potter tried to calm everyone down by reading aloud to them, but for once the class couldn't seem to concentrate as their teacher read *Tom Sawyer.* They wiggled and whispered and strained to look out the window at Maizie, who was just out of sight around a corner. When the principal appeared in their door and asked Mrs. Potter to come to his office, she threw up her hands and told the students to leave, even if it was ten minutes early.

Eddie stopped at the water fountain for a drink, which made him almost the last person out the back door. By the time he reached the playground, a big commotion was coming from near the Girl Scout float.

"That goat is eating our float!"

"Stop her, someone!"

"Grab her rope!"

The girls yelled, and the boys laughed. Maizie stood calmly in the middle of the turmoil, chewing on a tin can she had pulled off the float.

Eddie couldn't keep from laughing, too. Allen's grandmother had said that goats would eat anything, but he hadn't thought that meant tin cans, too.

"What are you laughing about?" Barb asked. She planted herself in front of her twin with her hands on her hips. "That animal is destroying our float."

Eddie laughed some more. "You've got to admit that it's pretty funny. A tin can, for Pete's sake."

"Stop her," Barb yelled.

"Oh, all right," Eddie said. "She can't hurt that float," he muttered as he joined Allen in grabbing Maizie's neck.

"What happened to her rope?" Eddie asked and looked around.

"I think this is all that's left," Allen said and held up a frayed scrap of rope. "I guess she ate all her grass and then the rope."

"I guess," Eddie agreed and grinned. "We've got to have some kind of rope." He looked around again. There were only angry girls and snickering boys. "Here, Warren, help Allen hold onto Maizie. I'll run inside and see if Mrs. Potter has any rope in the closet."

"Hurry up," Barb ordered.

Eddie did hurry. The other classes had emptied out, too, so the halls were quiet. Just as he dashed around the corner, an odd noise reached him. He stopped and listened, forgetting his mission. It came from his classroom, where the door stood part of the way open. He walked quietly up and peeked in the door. Mrs. Potter sat at her desk with her head down. The noise was the muffled sound of her crying.

Eddie backed up as a chill raced through him. He wasn't sure what to do. He didn't want to bother her, but should he try to help? What was wrong? He retreated into the hall as he tried to decide.

Steps sounded behind him, and he swung around to see Barb.

"Did you get the rope?" she demanded. "That goat got away again."

He put his finger over his lips to hush her. She frowned but obeyed. "What's wrong?" she whispered.

Eddie tiptoed over to the classroom door and motioned. "I don't know if we should go in or not," he whispered.

Barb peeked in the open door and looked back at her

brother, eyes wide with concern. They looked at each other for a moment before Barb said, "Come on, let's see if we can help."

They entered their classroom, which seemed unfamiliar when filled with the sound of their teacher weeping. Slowly they walked to Mrs. Potter, and Barb put her hand on the teacher's shoulder. "What's wrong? Can we help?"

Mrs. Potter raised a tear-stained face from her arms. Eddie felt like he might cry, too. "What's wrong, Mrs. Potter?" he repeated softly.

The tears ran freely down her face, but Eddie saw their teacher take a deep breath. "I'm sorry to cry." She swiped at her face with a hand and sniffed. "It's just that. . ." She hesitated, and the tears poured down her cheeks once again. "It's Donald. He's been killed. Shot down." Sobs shook her shoulders, and she placed her head on her arms once more.

Shock zapped through Eddie. The handsome pilot in the picture gone, just like that? How could that be? He knew men died in the war, lots of men, but surely not the kind of men who took time to write to kids. Not the kind of men who had wives as nice as Mrs. Potter.

Shock turned to anger. This wasn't fair. God wasn't fair if He let such things happen. He wanted to shake his fist and yell out his anger. But he didn't. Maybe later he could do that, but now all he could do was stand beside Barb, who was also crying. Behind them a breeze puffed in through the open windows and fluttered the flags that stuck out of their map. Eddie stared at that map, which would have one less flag and one more cross now. His eyes prickled, and a tear ran down his cheek.

CHAPTER 8

The Twins Turn Ten

The parade went on that day, but the sparkle was gone for all the students from Mrs. Potter's class. Maizie had cooperated as well as a goat could, and the girls had walked beside their float as the motorcycle pulled it slowly down the street. The principal had driven Mrs. Potter home after she had hugged Eddie and Barb and asked them to tell the others. It was a black day for Mrs. Potter's fourth-grade class.

But the days of fall went by, and eventually even Mrs. Potter's pale face perked up a little. Her students tried their best to behave, and she often told them how much it helped her feel better. Mr. Potter's flag on the map was the only one that had been switched to a cross so far. Eddie prayed every day that Steve's wouldn't be next.

The family had received occasional letters from Steve and they guessed he was still fighting in Italy. The letters had stopped abruptly at the end of October, which made everyone a bit uneasy. The radio announcer said that the fighting in Italy was fiercer and taking much longer than expected, but that the Allies were gaining ground foot by foot.

Mr. Lazarini still hadn't heard from his brother, and there was no news about Jim Watson. Eddie had heard his father say that no news was good news. Maybe that was the case with Jim and Steve and Mr. Lazarini's brother.

Guests moved in and out of the hotel, and always there were a million sheets to change and acres of floors to sweep and mop. Sal still lived with Mr. Lazarini, although as far as Eddie could tell, he only ate and slept at his cousin's house. Eddie thought the man only lived with Mr. Lazarini to eat the Italian man's cooking because Sal was definitely getting plumper.

Christmas was quiet for everyone. Eddie wondered if the others were remembering last Christmas when people were saying that the war would be over by the next year. Nobody said that now. This was the third Christmas that Steve had been gone, and Mama's face was solemn as the family bundled up to go to church on Christmas Eve.

Eddie planned to pray all the way through the service. He was over being mad at God, but he still didn't understand very much about this war. Mama had said that the Bible tells us to pray without ceasing, so that's what Eddie planned to do.

January started out cold and dreary. It was even rainier than usual, and the sun didn't peek out for days and days at a time. The twins plodded through their chores at the hotel, arguing every chance they got. All Eddie wanted was one sunny afternoon when he and Warren could go down to the waterfront, sit on the wharf, and watch the dockworkers unload ships. But it didn't happen because the rain just kept coming.

Then Alice caught a bad cold. She was sick for two weeks, and the others had to take over her work. Eddie didn't mind because his oldest sister had done his work many times, but he missed the only two sunny afternoons. By the time Alice was better, it was the end of January and the day of the twins' birthday.

"Do you think they've forgotten our birthday?" Barb asked. The twins were on cleanup duty again that Saturday morning. They were supposed to be sweeping the lobby and long hall-ways with two big dust mops that Dad had brought home last week.

"Maybe," Eddie said as they dragged the dust mops out of the closet.

"I didn't think Mama would forget," Barb said with a frown.

"Me either," Eddie said, "but maybe she'll remember later. Let's don't say anything for a while. If she still doesn't remember, we'll give her some hints."

"We could do that, couldn't we?" Barb's face perked up.

"Sure," Eddie said. "Come on, let's try out these new mops." He pushed at the long handle that ended with a mop head that looked like a huge gray mustache. "This is just like the janitor uses at school. When I was in first grade, I always wanted to ask him if I could get on the mop head part and ride while he pushed."

"Did you ever ask?"

"Nah. I was scared to talk to him."

Back and forth across the lobby they went, sweeping the dirt and tiny debris in front of them. The hard part was what to do with the dirt they swept up. Eddie had a feeling they were supposed to get the whisk broom and dustpan, but that was a lot of trouble. Instead, when they were sure no one was watching, they swept it out the front door and down the steps.

Eddie had just given his mop a hard shake outside at the bottom of the steps when a voice spoke up. "Excuse me. Do you know if Mr. Salvatorio Bolella lives in this hotel?"

Eddie jerked around and in doing so whacked his mop handle against the wall near where Barb stood with her mop. He flinched at the noise, and Barb ducked. "Sorry," he muttered to his sister before turning to the owner of the voice.

A young woman stood on the sidewalk. Eddie realized that she was pretty, but that wasn't what he noticed most of all. She was dressed in black from head to toe. She wore a long coat with a slouchy kind of hat and odd-looking black boots. A cigarette dangled from her fingertips at the end of a sticklike holder. The only touch of color was her lips, and they were covered with bloodred lipstick.

"Salvatorio?" Eddie asked with a frown.

"You must mean Sal," Barb said and pushed Eddie aside. "He lives at the top of the stairs in the last hallway off the lobby. It's apartment four."

"Thank you," the woman in black said and made her way up the stairs.

"Interesting," Barb said.

"I wonder what she wants with Sal?" Eddie asked.

"Just a friend, I suppose," Barb answered and started up the stairs, too.

Eddie lifted his eyebrows but didn't say anything. This woman might be one more clue in the mystery of Sal, or she might be collecting for some charity. If that were the case, she'd be out of luck with Sal.

The twins carried their mops to the closest hallway.

"Let's get this done. I'm tired of looking at dirt," Barb said.

Eddie bent over to pick up a piece of paper that lay on the floor near the apartment where Donnie lived with his father. "Look," he said and held it out for Barb to see. "It's a movie star picture."

"It's Lana Turner," Barb said after looking at the picture.

"I know," Eddie said. He thought Lana Turner was pretty, but he'd keep that thought to himself since Barb was likely to laugh.

"I wonder how it got in the hall?" Barb asked.

"I think it's Donnie's," Eddie answered. "I've seen it in his school notebook before. Lots of the older boys have pictures of movie stars."

"He should be more careful with it," Barb said. "She is pretty, but I like Clark Gable better. I saw him on a newsreel last week at the movies."

"I saw Lana Turner on one, too, a couple of weeks ago," Eddie said and put the picture on a nearby ledge. "She was talking to some soldiers."

"I guess all those movie stars try to help out with the war effort," Barb said. She sighed. "I wish Clark Gable would help out here."

"Forget movie stars," Eddie said. "We've still got one more

hallway to sweep." They carried their mops through the lobby. The last hallway stretched out endlessly before them.

"Let's race," Eddie proposed. "We'll see who can get their mop to the end of the hall and back first. The sweeping will be done, and we'll know who's the fastest." He said this last with a wide smile and waited for Barb to bristle up.

"That won't be any contest," Barb said quickly. "I may be little, but my feet aren't nearly as big as yours. I won't be getting tangled up like you probably will."

"We'll just see about that," Eddie said. "Come over here and make a starting line."

"I wish we had someone to say *go*," Barb said. She lifted her mop and went over to the end of the hall.

"Well, we don't," Eddie said, "unless you want to ask Mama." He was teasing because their mother was likely to take a dim view of another race.

"I guess that won't be necessary," Barb said and stuck her tongue out at her twin.

They lined up and Eddie said, "Ready, set, go!" Off they went, flying down the hallway, with their mops in front. Eddie was a little ahead when they made the turnaround at the end, but he caught his mop for a second on a broken edge of the linoleum, slowing him down. He turned on the speed to catch up and had almost accomplished that when Mrs. Hunter opened her door and stepped out into the hall. She was dressed in her good black coat and hat, with her handbag over her arm. Her head was ducked down a little as she tucked something in her pocket.

Eddie saw their neighbor but quickly realized that Barb didn't. His twin had turned her head toward him, probably to see how far ahead she was. He opened his mouth to yell, but it was too late. Barb crashed into Mrs. Hunter, who saw the girl just in time to avoid being bowled over but not in time to keep her purse from going one direction and her hat the other as she tried to move out of the way. Barb ended up on the floor with a thud.

Eddie dropped his mop and hurried to help Barb up and get Mrs. Hunter's bag and hat. "Are you all right?" he asked the older woman and then his sister.

Barb nodded and looked nervously at Mrs. Hunter, who seemed to be gathering up steam to speak.

"I am just fine, I assure you," the woman said and yanked her handbag and hat away from Eddie. "No thanks to you two young hooligans."

"We're sorry," Eddie began. "We were sweeping the floor."

"Spare me the details," Mrs. Hunter said with a loud sniff as she jammed her hat back on her head. "You're both incorrigible, and your mother shall hear about this." She gave a final sniff and stalked off down the hall, her back stiff and her chin held high.

"What's incorrigible?" Eddie asked.

"I don't know, but I don't think it's something that Mama is going to take kindly to," Barb answered. "We'll be in trouble for sure, and on our birthdays. This is all your fault. If you hadn't wanted to race, I wouldn't have run into her."

"You should have watched where you were going," Eddie said and beat a hasty retreat down the hall with his mop.

"Eddie, Barb, come quick," Audrey yelled from the hotel lobby.

"That was fast," Eddie said with a frown. Getting in trouble didn't seem to take any time at all these days. He put away his mop and dashed toward the office, leaving Barb to catch up.

Might as well get this over with. He slowed as he approached the office and put on what he thought of as his *sorry* face. It couldn't hurt, and he was sorry—even though Mrs. Hunter was a grouch sometimes.

"Where's Barb?" Mama asked. Her eyes sparkled but not with anger. She was excited. Eddie looked around a moment before answering, but Mrs. Hunter was nowhere to be seen.

"She's coming," Eddie said. He forgot about looking sorry because apparently he wasn't in trouble yet. "What's going on?"

"Wait for Barb," his mother said.

Then Eddie saw that she had an envelope in her hand. It looked like the kind of envelope that Steve always used. "Is it a letter from Steve?"

Mama nodded, her smile wide. "Barb," she hollered down the hall, "hurry up."

"Go ahead and open it," Eddie said.

"No, it's addressed to you and Barb," Mama said. "For your birthday, I imagine. After no letters for weeks and weeks, your birthday letter manages to get here on the right day. It's God's gift."

Barb arrived, and they all crowded around to listen as she read Steve's letter aloud. Written on Christmas afternoon, Steve's letter had evidently been missed by the censors because there were no cutouts where words had been removed. He didn't say directly where he was, but he talked about trying Yorkshire pudding and going to church at a big cathedral and about the day after Christmas being called Boxing Day. Mama said it sounded to her like he was in England. She said that other letters written before this one would probably arrive soon, and they might mention that he had moved to a different place.

"England will be safe, won't it?" Eddie asked.

"I should think it would be much safer than Italy," Mama replied, "and much more comfortable, too. There's no ground fighting there."

"Why would he be sent there?" Audrey asked. "They don't use tanks in England."

"I can't answer that," Mama said. "Maybe it's only temporary." Her face sobered for a moment. "But we're not going to think about that now." She smiled at the twins. "We're going to have a celebration. We've heard from Steve, and it's the twins' birthday. Time for a party."

Eddie and Barb cheered and danced around their mother and then around Audrey and Alice.

"Did you think we'd forgotten your birthdays?" Mama asked Eddie a little later.

"Maybe," Eddie admitted. "We wondered, anyhow."

"I could never forget the day I got the biggest surprise of my life," Mama said and put her arm on Eddie's shoulders. "Two babies when I was only expecting one. It was the best surprise ever."

That evening after Dad and Isabel came home from Boeing, they all gathered in the apartment living room to celebrate. Mr. Lazarini and Aunt Daisy came, too, and they all ate big bowls of ham and beans with cornbread. Aunt Daisy had used her meat points to get a nice chunk of ham, and Mr. Lazarini had baked the best cornbread Eddie had ever eaten. After they had finished the beans, Mama disappeared into the kitchen and in a few moments came back triumphantly carrying a big cake.

"It's chocolate," she announced to the twins. "We've been

saving sugar and cocoa a little at a time for weeks. Happy birthday."

Eddie felt his mouth water. He missed sweets more than anything else that was in short supply during the war. He thought he could eat this cake all by himself, but of course he wouldn't, since everyone else's mouth was probably watering, too.

They ate cake and talked about Steve's letter, and then, as usual, the talk turned to the war. Eddie felt full and happy as he listened to Dad and Mr. Lazarini and Aunt Daisy talk about how much longer the war could last. The war was terrible, but sometimes there were happy times, and this night was one of them.

"It turned out to be a great birthday, right, brother?" Barb asked as she lowered herself to the floor near Eddie. They sat a little apart from the others.

"Sure did," Eddie agreed. "I wasn't too sure it would after this morning."

Barb frowned. "In all the excitement of the letter, I almost forgot that," she said. "Did Mama say anything to you about the mop problem?"

Eddie shook his head. "No, but maybe she's waiting to punish us until after our birthday is over."

"Or maybe Mrs. Hunter didn't tell her."

The twins looked at each other for a moment. It was another time when they didn't have to talk out loud to know what the other one was thinking.

"Mama says Mrs. Hunter has a real sweet tooth," Barb said.

"There's a piece of cake left," Eddie added.

"It was for us to split."

Eddie sighed. "I know." He got up from the floor. Talk and

laughter vibrated in the living room as everyone offered opinions on every possible subject. He loved family gatherings. "Come on." He motioned to Barb.

In a few minutes they were at Mrs. Hunter's door, knocking. She opened the door and frowned at the twins.

Barb held out the piece of cake that they had placed on a plate and carefully covered with a napkin. "This is for you, Mrs. Hunter."

"It's from our birthday cake," Eddie added.

"We're really sorry about this morning," Barb said.

"We'll be more careful from now on," Eddie said. He watched the woman's face and saw surprise and something else there.

Slowly Mrs. Hunter reached out and took the cake. "Well, I should hope so," she said acidly, but her voice softened when she lifted the napkin and looked at the peace offering. "Oh, I do so love chocolate cake."

"It's delicious," Eddie said.

Barb nodded. "Our mother is the best cook ever."

A real smile lit up Mrs. Hunter's face for the first time that Eddie could remember. She looked much younger and sort of pretty.

"We better go," Barb said.

"Thank you, children," Mrs. Hunter said, "and happy birthday."

The twins tramped back down the hall toward their own apartment where the celebration could still be heard.

"I sure would have liked to eat more cake," Eddie admitted.

"Me, too," Barb agreed.

"Maybe by the time we're eleven, the war will be over,"

Eddie said. "And we'll have cake and cookies and pudding and fudge and. . ."

"Steak and licorice and. . ."

"We don't like licorice," Eddie interrupted.

"We might by the time we're eleven," Barb said, "so we want there to be plenty."

"You're right," Eddie said. "And peppermints. . ."

"And gasoline and tires so we can go to the country again."

They walked down the hall trying to think up all the things that they might have next year. For once the twins were in perfect agreement.

CHAPTER 9

The Junk Car

At last the long rainy winter had passed, and May brought a series of sunshiny days perfect for scrap metal prospecting. This year's Victory garden had been planted but didn't need to be weeded yet, so Eddie and Warren had planned a whole Saturday to look for scrap.

There was to be a big rally on June 12 to celebrate the beginning of the fifth war loan drive, and that same day would be the end of a scrap metal drive that had started last week. Eddie and Warren planned to show the girls how this collecting business should be done.

"What do you hear from Steve these days?" Warren asked as the pair started out Saturday morning after chores were finished. The plan was to crisscross the streets and alleys south of Yesler, looking for metal of any kind. They each carried old burlap bags for their finds.

"We've had lots of letters from him lately," Eddie replied. "I don't think he has much to do in England." He stopped for a moment to peer around a building corner. The alley was bare except for two cats sunning on a stoop.

"Why is he still there?"

Eddie shrugged his shoulders. "Don't know. At least not for sure. Dad says that sooner or later the Allies will invade Europe. He doesn't say it, but I think he wonders if Steve is waiting to do that." Eddie had a feeling that Dad didn't talk much about that because of Mama. She had been so cheerful this winter just knowing that Steve was in England.

The boys walked and talked and looked for close to an hour. Finally Warren lifted up an old tarp that lay in a corner near the back door of a warehouse. "Nothing here, either. We've been looking forever and don't have a single piece of scrap that amounts to anything." He dumped his sack and a rusted piece of bucket tumbled out.

"You're right," Eddie said. All he had in his sack was a mashed toy car. "We've had so many scrap drives that I guess there's not much left."

"We'll never win the contest at this rate," Warren said. "What about the girls? Are they collecting today, too?"

"They went with Frank back to our old house. Barb said that Frank wanted to get something out of the shed, but I think they're looking for scrap." Eddie leaned over to pick up a long bolt that he saw in the gutter.

"That doesn't seem fair," Warren said. "It's your house, too."

Eddie grinned. "I checked it out last week when I went with Alice to collect the rent and get Mama's good tablecloth out of the box in the attic. There's nothing there any better than this junk." He ran into the street to pick up a squashed old teapot that lay there.

"I guess it all adds up," Warren said.

"Yeah, but not fast enough to win that contest. We need something big."

"Like what?" Warren asked.

"I don't know," Eddie said. He stopped for a moment. "Something like a machine that isn't any good anymore."

"Where would we find that?"

"Not around here. That's for sure," Eddie said. "Maybe we should get on the bus and go farther south, where there are more houses instead of apartments or even farther where there're factories."

"Couldn't hurt," Warren said. "We could go out near Boeing. It's not that far, really."

A quick trip back to the hotel got them some lunch and permission from Mama to go if they'd be back before dark. A half-hour later they were on the bus headed south.

"I haven't been out here since the plane crash last year," Eddie said. He hadn't thought about that crash in a long time. He wondered again if the woman who had called for Albert had ever found him.

"Let's get off at the next stop," Warren said in a little while. "We're almost to the Boeing factory. We can circle around and see what we can find."

They pulled the bell and climbed off the bus at the next corner.

"Tell me again what we're looking for," Warren said after they had walked a block.

"We'll know it when we see it."

Warren raised his eyebrows. "Maybe you will, but I need a little more to go on."

Eddie laughed. "Come on, let's look over there." He pointed to an overgrown vacant lot across the street. It looked a little like the Victory garden lot before they had plowed it up, but the grass and weeds were much taller. Eddie doubted he and Warren could see over the tops, even though they were both pretty tall for their age.

"You really want to go in that jungle?" Warren asked doubtfully. The boys crossed the street and stood at the edge of the lot.

"It doesn't look like anyone else has been in there lately, either," Eddie said. "Who knows what we might find?"

"Snakes and bugs," Warren muttered.

Eddie waded in the weeds a few feet. "Look here, a bunch of little paths. Probably made by small animals."

"Wild animals! In Seattle!" Warren stopped abruptly.

"I didn't say wild," Eddie said. "They might be dog trails or rabbit tunnels."

"Oh," Warren said sheepishly.

The boys pushed through the tall weeds, following the paths that crossed the big lot. Every so often, Eddie stopped and looked around. Toward the rear of the lot was a stand of brushy trees, and he gradually led them closer to that area.

"What's that big lump over there?" Warren asked the next time they stopped. He pointed to the right.

Eddie strained his eyes in that direction. There was a big

brownish something in the thicket of trees. He pushed closer. "It looks like. . ."

"A junk car," Warren finished for Eddie.

Sure enough, the rusting hulk of an old car rose out of the weeds and brush. Silly as it seemed, it looked to Eddie as if it had grown there. The tires had long since flattened into puddles of rotted rubber, and the rust patches made the light brown paint look spotted.

"Wow! This would make a ton of scrap," Eddie said.

"Are you crazy?" Warren asked. "How could we get this out of here, and who does it belong to anyway?"

"Problems to be solved, that's all," Eddie answered, and a big grin spread across his face. "It could be done."

"I guess nobody must want it or it wouldn't be rusting away out here," Warren conceded.

"We'd try to find the owner." But Eddie couldn't imagine any owner who wouldn't be glad to get rid of such a big piece of junk.

"How would we get it to the collection center?" Warren pushed through the brush to look at the front of the old heap. "The girls could never find something this big. We'd be bound to win the contest." His eyes lit up.

"I was thinking the same thing," Eddie said. "Not that it matters, of course." He peeked inside the broken side window of the car. The back seat's stuffing had been pulled out and scattered. "Looks like some field mice have been living in here. I guess they'll have to move."

"If we can figure out how to get it out of this lot," Warren said.

"Oh, we'll think of something. We always do."

The boys backtracked through the weeds to the street and started the trek to the bus stop, talking all the way.

"We'd need some way to pull it out of that lot," Eddie said.

"Once it was out, maybe it could be dragged to the collection center," Warren said.

"A tow truck is what we need," Eddie said, "but where could we come up with that?"

Warren stopped short and snapped his fingers. "Carolyn's father has some kind of a winch on his truck. It's like what they use on tow trucks. I think he just puts it on when he needs to lift or haul something for his job."

"We could ask him if he'd help," Eddie said. "He probably would. He's done lots of war work around the neighborhood."

"Only one problem," Warren said and started walking again.

"Yeah," Eddie said. "The girls. We'd have to tell the girls, and we'd have to share the scrap." The pair walked in silence for a few minutes.

"Maybe we could make a deal," Warren said. "Give them some of the credit, but we get more because we found it."

"Maybe," Eddie said doubtfully. Barb was way too intent on winning this contest to agree to any kind of deal.

"Look, there's Boeing," Warren said. The huge factory complex sat off to one side with parking lots around it. "I heard that the roof is camouflaged to look like a little town."

"I couldn't say," Eddie said. The war made lots of talk off limits, and the fact that the big airplane factory had been disguised to look like a village fell in that category. Sometimes Eddie let himself think what would happen if the enemy managed to find out important things about Boeing, like how it was camouflaged or what kind of planes it made. Maybe they'd do something drastic to try to get rid of the factory. That was a scary thought.

"We sure can't see anything from here," Warren said.

"Too far away from the main buildings," Eddie agreed. They were near the front gate of the complex, which was guarded by several security guards. Outside the gate, men and women milled around, waiting for buses or other rides. Dad said there were always people coming and going because of the different shifts for different production lines.

"Maybe we can catch the bus here," Warren said.

Eddie nodded. He was tired of walking. They pushed through the crowd until they found a sign for the bus they needed.

"Let's wait right here," Eddie said and sank down on the street curb.

The pair sat quietly for a few minutes just looking and listening. A couple of buses arrived and departed while Eddie and Warren watched.

Eddie's eye was caught by a familiar figure that stood in a group of uniformed workers across the street. He jabbed Warren in the ribs. "Look at that! Over there."

"Well, what do you know," Warren said. "It's good old Sal."

Sure enough, Mr. Lazarini's cousin was talking earnestly to a couple of Boeing workers. As the boys watched, Sal led the pair over to a black car parked on the street nearby. All three climbed into the back seat of the car, but the car didn't pull away.

"What he's doing?" Eddie asked. "He doesn't have a car that I know of. And why isn't he at work at the shipyard?"

"It's not the first time he's skipped work," Warren said.

"I was up early this morning and saw him leave for work with his lunch pail." Eddie watched as the two Boeing workers climbed out of the car and walked away. In a minute another worker walked up and stuck his head in the open back door of the car, then climbed in and shut the door. What was Sal up to?

Another figure approached the car but didn't open the door. It was the woman Eddie had seen before, the one dressed in black who had asked for Sal at the hotel. This time she still wore black but without the long coat and hat. A cigarette dangled once more from a holder she grasped loosely between her fingers, and she leaned against the car's fender.

"Is she with Sal?" Warren leaned over to talk in Eddie's ear.

"I've seen her before," Eddie replied and told Warren about the woman coming to the hotel.

As they watched, the worker climbed out of the back seat, followed by Sal. The woman in black walked over to Sal, who opened the front car door for her. She slid in, and Sal started around the car. Just then another man in a Boeing uniform stopped him.

About the same time the bus pulled up at the stop. With a last glance at Mr. Lazarini's cousin, Eddie and Warren climbed aboard.

"Quick," Eddie said. "Get that seat over there." He pointed to an empty seat halfway back on the bus. They tumbled into their place and scrambled to stick their heads out the window. Sal was still talking to the worker. As the bus slowly pulled away from the curb, Eddie saw the man shove something into Sal's hand and receive some kind of paper in return. Someone shouted from behind Eddie and Warren on the bus. Sal's head jerked up at the sound, and in the next instant he looked straight at the bus.

"Duck!" Eddie yelled, and the boys fell back to the seat and stared at each other.

"Do you think he saw us?" Eddie asked. In a moment he sat up enough to peek out the window again as the bus picked up speed. "He's still looking."

"I don't think so," Warren said. "I think he was looking at the back. What was that all about?"

"I don't know for sure," Eddie answered. There was just so much about Sal that didn't make sense. What was he doing with the Boeing workers, and why was that woman with him? He frowned as he remembered the paper that had changed hands, the paper that looked like a folded envelope. What could a Boeing worker be giving to Sal?

There were so many questions and no answers. At the back of Eddie's mind, a prickly thought kept coming back. What if the Boeing workers were giving Sal information about the factory? Was it possible that Mr. Lazarini's cousin was a spy?

CHAPTER 10

More Clues

Eddie and Warren had a lot to mull over for the next week or so. They traipsed through neighborhood after neighborhood, looking for scrap that would be easier to retrieve than the old car. It seemed there wasn't any decent scrap metal left anywhere in Seattle. The other Boy Scouts complained of the same problem and said they were going to collect newspapers instead. Eddie and Warren weren't ready to give up yet, especially when Barb and Carolyn gave no sign of quitting.

Eddie couldn't stop thinking about Sal and the woman in black and the Boeing workers. He wanted to go right up to Sal and ask him what he had been doing at the Boeing gate, but he was pretty sure that wasn't the way to approach a spy, because Eddie had decided that the facts pointed in that direction. No, a better plan would be to do a little spying himself with Sal as the object. To do that he needed to talk to Mr. Lazarini alone.

"If it isn't my good friend Eddie," Mr. Lazarini said with a broad smile when he opened his front door the following Friday. "Come in and have a piece of biscotti. It's freshly baked."

"Sounds great," Eddie said and sat down at Mr. Lazarini's tiny kitchen table.

"I haven't seen you for a week or more," Mr. Lazarini said as he placed a plate of biscotti in front of Eddie. "You've been a busy boy."

Eddie nodded and chewed his cookie. Mr. Lazarini pulled a milk bottle out of the small refrigerator and motioned to it. Eddie nodded again and gratefully took the glass of milk he was handed. When he could talk he said, "School was out for the summer this week and there was lots of school stuff. How have you been?" Now that Eddie was here to check up on Sal, he wasn't sure how to go about it.

"I'm just fine," Mr. Lazarini replied. "I love this sunny weather we've been having almost as much as my geraniums do." He nodded his head in the direction of the window where geraniums and other plants stretched toward the afternoon sun.

"Does Sal like the sunny weather, too?" Eddie asked. It seemed as good a way as any to switch the conversation to the cousin.

"Can't say that Sal notices things like sunshine all that much," Mr. Lazarini said. A slight shadow passed over his face at the mention of his cousin. "Besides, he spends most of his time indoors when the sun is out."

"Is he still on the day shift?" Eddie was sure he knew the answer, but a detective should double-check his facts.

"Has been for months now," Mr. Lazarini replied. "Lately he's been working twelve-hour shifts again."

"Does he work on Saturdays, too?"

"All the time. I think most shipyard workers do," Mr. Lazarini said. "Say, you're awful interested in old Sal's schedule. How come?"

Eddie shrugged and grinned at his friend. "Just wondering, that's all." He didn't want to say anything to Mr. Lazarini about Sal's comings and goings until he knew more facts.

"So tell me about the latest contest with the girls," Mr. Lazarini said. "Knowing you children as I do, I'm sure there is one."

Eddie took one last drink of milk before telling Mr. Lazarini about the junk car and his hopes to get it for the scrap drive. The older man listened and nodded once in awhile.

"So what do you think?" Eddie asked. "Do you have any ideas about getting that car to the collection center?"

"Sounds to me like you already have a good idea," Mr. Lazarini said. "Carolyn's father would be your best bet. I've met him before at Civil Defense meetings. I think he'd help you."

"But then we'd have to let the girls in on the plan and probably have to share the scrap with them, too."

"So you said," Mr. Lazarini replied, "but maybe it's more important to get all that scrap for the war effort than it is to beat the girls. At least you should think about it."

"I will," Eddie promised as he got up to leave. Getting the old car was one thing, but what about Sal? Catching a spy would be even more important for the war effort, but Eddie was a long way from having enough information to do that.

Memorial Day was the following Tuesday, and he still didn't know anything more about Sal by then. Warren had gone to visit some cousins before they could decide what to do about the car, but he'd be back for Tuesday's ceremonies. Then they'd decide what to do.

Tuesday turned out to be yet another sunny day, perfect for all the Memorial Day observances that were planned all over Seattle. Eddie dressed carefully in his Boy Scout uniform about noon and went with Barb, who was in her Girl Scout uniform as well, to meet the rest of the family in the hotel lobby. Even Dad and Isabel had a half-day off from work. Donnie's dad had volunteered to watch the office so the whole Harrington family could attend. Aunt Daisy and Mr. Lazarini had gone on ahead in Aunt Daisy's car to save a place for their picnic.

"Don't you two look official," Dad said. He and Frank and Isabel stood by the office door.

"I get to carry a flag in the procession," Eddie said proudly.

"My troop will be there, too," Barb said.

"But without flags," Eddie said and saw his twin make a face.

"No arguing from either of you," Mama said as she came out of the office door. Behind her, Alice and Audrey carried two picnic hampers. "This is a day for us to enjoy being together."

"And honor our fighting men and women," Dad added. He took Alice's hamper from her, and Frank took Audrey's. In a few minutes the family was out the door and squeezing into the DeSoto for the trip to the cemetery.

"Why is the Memorial Day ceremony held at the cemetery?" Barb asked.

"Yeah," Eddie said, "why is that? A cemetery doesn't seem

like the right place for a celebration." He had thought about that last night before he went to sleep. A cemetery was a place of death, but they were going there for a picnic.

"Depends on how you look at it," Dad said over his shoulder as he steered through the traffic. "We're celebrating our country and what it stands for, but we're also honoring the men and women who have died to protect it."

"I have a few flowers in the hamper to decorate some graves," Mama said. "I'm just sorry that it's too soon for our Victory garden zinnias to be in bloom."

"But we don't know anyone who is buried in this cemetery," Barb said.

"It doesn't matter," Mama said. "We'll just decorate some graves that don't have any flowers already."

Eddie leaned back in the seat where he sat wedged in between Frank and Barb. He wondered if Mrs. Potter was decorating her husband's grave today. Their teacher had moved the day after school dismissed for the summer. She had gone back to her hometown in Missouri, the place where she had met her husband. Eddie thought about that for a few moments before he remembered that Mrs. Potter couldn't decorate her husband's grave. His body hadn't been brought back to the United States.

It didn't take long to get to the cemetery, but they had to park a long way from the platform that had been built for the ceremony.

"Eddie," a voice hollered, "over here." Warren waved at Eddie from behind a stone wall that surrounded a group of graves. Eddie hurried over to join the rest of his Boy Scout troop.

"We thought you weren't going to make it," Warren said. "It's almost time to start."

"We had to wait for Dad and Isabel," Eddie said. "Where do I stand?"

"Here," Warren said and handed Eddie a small American flag. "Walk behind me."

A band up ahead began to play, and the boys fell into step. They marched up the center aisle between crowds of people who sat on wooden folding chairs. When they got to the platform, they stopped and lined either side of the stairs. Eddie saw Barb and Carolyn with the other Girl Scouts off to one side of the platform, where they stood in salute to the flags.

The dignitaries marched down the aisle and up the steps between Eddie and Warren and the others. Eddie saw several older men in military uniforms, World War I veterans, he was sure, and two younger uniformed men. One of them was on crutches and slowly made his way up the steps while the other young man walked beside him. The second man's uniform coat sleeve was empty, pinned up so it wouldn't dangle. Both men must be wounded veterans of this war, Steve's war.

Bringing up the rear were a couple of other men in suits. One of them was the Reverend Colston. The preacher grinned at Eddie before mounting the platform. After all the dignitaries were lined up on the stage, the Boy Scouts filed down to stand in front of chairs on the front row, and the band finished with a flourish.

The ceremony got under way with the Pledge of Allegiance, after which everyone sank into the chairs. There were speeches from the older veterans and speeches from the young ones. Finally the talking was over, and Eddie sat up straighter. It was time for the reading of the roll of honor. That job had been given to Pastor Colston.

He read the names of soldiers from Seattle who had been killed in the past year. His deep voice hesitated between each name as if to give that soldier his due. It was a long list, but no one in the audience stirred. At last Eddie heard what he had been waiting for, *Donald Edward Potter, Army Air Corps.* He had made sure that Mr. Potter was on Pastor Colston's list.

The last name hung in the air for a moment before the sound of a bugle pierced the silence. Eddie tilted his head to listen. It was coming from a little hill among the gravestones a hundred yards away. Eddie had heard Taps played before but never like this. His heart felt torn apart as he listened to the clear notes of the bugle that surged across the cemetery. It played in honor of Mr. Potter, Carolyn's brother, and all the others, dead in countries far from the one they defended. The bugle seemed to hold all that pain and send it floating out over the crowd. As the last note faded, Eddie heard sniffs and sighs all around him and some quiet sobbing, too.

Then it was over, and everyone began to talk and laugh and look for their picnic baskets. Eddie realized that he was starved, and he and Warren set off to find their families.

Mama and Alice had spread a couple of blankets on the grass near the platform. Many other people had done the same, so there was a big crowd. Warren's family joined the Harringtons, and in a minute Carolyn and her family came up to spread their blanket next to the others. Aunt Daisy and Mr. Lazarini were already settled and pulling food out of their hampers. It was a great big party, and Eddie feasted happily on fried chicken, potato salad, pickles, and lots of other goodies. He and Warren had to lie back on the blanket to rest before they could dig into the cake that Warren's mother had brought.

"Got room for a hungry fellow?" a voice asked from the other side of the blanket. Eddie recognized that voice.

"Sure thing, Sal," Dad said. "Sit down and dig in." Dad scooted over to make room for the neighbor.

"I thought you had to work," Mr. Lazarini said to his cousin as he handed him a plate. Sal took the plate and heaped it with food.

"Got off early for the holiday," Sal answered around a mouthful of potato salad. "Didn't want to miss the ceremonies honoring our soldiers."

"Likely story," Eddie whispered to Warren. "He probably didn't want to miss a good meal."

Warren snickered. "He's not missing anything."

The boys watched as Sal loaded up his plate a second and then a third time. Eddie shook his head. It was a good thing that Mama had fried that extra chicken and brought more rolls than she had first planned.

"We better get our cake," Warren said, "or there won't be any left."

After eating, Eddie and Warren wandered off to look at gravestones and read the inscriptions that were carved on the stones. It made Eddie feel funny at first to walk among the graves, some of which had been carefully decorated with flowers, but soon he and Warren were going from one to the other to look at the names and dates.

"This man was ninety-five when he died," Eddie said after some quick arithmetic in his head.

"This woman was ninety-nine," Warren said from in front of a tall stone with flowers carved on the top.

"Women always live longer than men," Barb said and

popped out from behind the stone, followed by Carolyn.

"That's not true," Eddie said. At least he didn't think it was true, but he wouldn't let Barb know he had any doubt.

"We'll prove it," Barb said and grabbed Carolyn's hand. "We'll find two or three women who died when they were a hundred years old or more. You won't find a single man that old."

"That's where you're wrong," Eddie said. "Come on, Warren, let's show these girls that men always win."

"Even in the graveyard," Warren added with a laugh.

They ran from stone to stone, weaving across the cemetery, careful to avoid the flowers. Calling out dates to each other, they searched for the oldest occupants.

"Here's a man who was ninety-nine," Warren called from the front of a huge gravestone.

"So was this woman," Carolyn yelled.

"Doesn't count," Barb said. "They have to be at least a hundred."

They worked their way farther apart until Eddie ended up by himself near a group of identical gravestones. They were much smaller than most of the other stones and worn by age. Curious, he walked closer to read the inscriptions. It was one family. Stone after stone revealed that the Anderson children had died within days of each other in 1918. Eddie remembered reading in school about a big flu epidemic that killed thousands of people that year. Two stones at the very end proved to be soldiers who died in World War I about the same time as the children. No doubt they were older brothers.

"What are you looking at?" Warren asked as he walked up. "Did you find a real old one?"

"No," Eddie said, "just the opposite." He waved to the row of stones. "They all died too young."

Warren stared at the names and dates as Eddie had done. "I see what you mean."

"Why does God do that?" Eddie asked. "Why does He let a whole family die?" He didn't really expect Warren to have an answer, but he just had to say it out loud. There was so much about life and death that he questioned these days.

"You're asking the wrong person," Warren said, "because I don't know." He reached down and gently brushed a pile of leaves away from the base of one of the stones. "Why don't you ask God? He's the one in charge and the one with the answers."

"How would He answer?" Eddie asked.

"My mother says that He finds a way," Warren answered, "and I think she's right. Sometimes when I pray about something, like a problem or a choice, the answer will come to me."

"Like magic?"

"No, it's not like that," Warren replied. "It's quieter, and it usually takes longer. Sometimes I'm not even sure if it's God talking to me, but most of the time I can tell, if I'm paying attention."

"I'll try it," Eddie said. And he would, too. He had lots of questions he wanted to ask God.

Voices rang across the graves, angry voices raised in argument. Eddie and Warren turned at the same time. Not far away stood three figures behind a small square marble building. Eddie strained his eyes and ears in the strangers' direction. He saw a woman and two men, and they weren't strangers after all, at least not all of them.

The woman he had seen twice before with Sal, the woman

in black. She stood with Mr. Lazarini's cousin and again wore black. Sal and the other man were arguing, but Eddie couldn't hear any words clearly. The other man was taller than Sal and quite skinny compared to Sal's portly build.

With no hesitation, Eddie motioned to Warren to follow him as he circled around to get closer to the trio. Maybe the mystery of Sal could be solved if he could hear what the two men were arguing about. At least it might be a clue.

It wasn't hard to sneak up on Sal and the others, because they all were talking at once. Several large gravestones dotted the area near the marble building, so it was just a question of getting from one to the other without being seen. In a matter of moments Eddie and Warren were close enough to understand the voices.

"If you can't deliver the goods, I'll get someone else," the tall man said. "You're not the only one of your kind in Seattle. That I can say for sure."

"Don't get so excited," Sal said. "I said I'd deliver, and I will. I've got another contact to make before I can get everything sewed up. My man is on the day shift at Number Two and needs some persuasion."

"Get him on board or get rid of him," the tall man said. "I want to see something concrete by Saturday, no later. I'll be around to visit you then."

"I'm in the underground now," Sal said. "She'll show you."

"Depend on it," the tall man said and jerked his head at the woman. "Let's go. This place gives me the willies."

Eddie watched as the trio split up. Sal walked back toward the picnic area, and the other two headed in the opposite direction.

"What were they talking about?" Warren asked after a moment or two. The boys sank down to sit on the ground at the base of a big stone.

Eddie shook his head. "I'm not sure, but it didn't sound good at all. Was he talking about getting information from someone? They call the Boeing factory Number Two."

"Maybe it was something else."

"Maybe," Eddie agreed, "but what?" He frowned as the men's words ran through his mind again and again. They had talked about delivering the goods and using persuasion. It had to be spying, didn't it?

"What are you two doing here?" Barb demanded. "You're supposed to be looking for hundred-year-old men."

Eddie jumped at his sister's voice. He had totally forgotten their interrupted search.

"We got sidetracked," Warren said.

"Yeah, that's right," Eddie agreed.

"Was that Sal I saw walking back toward the picnic area?" Barb asked. "What's he doing out here?" she added after Eddie nodded.

"I don't know," Eddie said and gave Warren a warning look. He didn't want to tell Barb about Sal and everything that they had heard. She'd want to take over and tell him just what to do. He wasn't sure what to do next, but he knew he didn't need his sister to boss him around.

"That fellow's hiding something," Barb said before changing the subject. "So did you find any hundred-year-old men?"

Warren and Barb began a good-natured argument about the search, but Eddie couldn't take his mind off Sal. The tall man had said he'd be back on Saturday. If what Eddie heard was really what he thought he'd heard, there were only four days before Sal was going to deliver some valuable information about Boeing. Only four days to catch a spy!

CHAPTER 11

The Spy's Lair

"Eddie, what in the world is the matter with you?" Mama asked on Friday afternoon. "You're not my cheerful boy this week. In fact, you've been downright grouchy. Is something wrong?" Mama was sorting sheets in the laundry room while Eddie stacked towels on the shelves.

"Not exactly," Eddie replied. "I'm fine." He smiled as big

as he could at his mother. He knew he had been touchy ever since Tuesday.

"Well, if you can't tell me about it," Mama said, "be sure to tell God. He can help."

Eddie nodded and grabbed more towels to stack. He had been telling God, begging Him, in fact, to show him what to do about Sal. But so far God hadn't answered.

Eddie and Warren hadn't been able to find out a thing about Sal all week. Eddie had gotten up early and gone to bed late trying to keep an eye on Sal, with no luck. The man slipped in and out of the hotel like a ghost. Tomorrow was the deadline the tall man from the cemetery had set, and they weren't any closer to catching Sal. It was enough to make anyone grouchy.

At last the hotel chores were done, and Eddie waited for Warren in the lobby. It was time for a new plan. Eddie wished he had one to offer.

"I thought we'd be able to follow him," Eddie said a few minutes later after Warren had arrived. They scooted Mittens over and sat down on the old couch in the lobby. "We'd follow him and see where his place is, the one he said was in the underground. Once we could prove what he's doing, we'd report him to the authorities."

"Do you think that's where his spy stuff is?" Warren asked.

"It must be. There isn't room in Mr. Lazarini's apartment for anything like that."

"What do spies have anyhow?"

"Probably radio equipment," Eddie said, "and maybe files or notebooks."

"Why doesn't he live there? Why does he bother coming back to the hotel every day?" Warren asked.

"It's his cover," Eddie said firmly. "Who'd suspect a chubby Italian shipyard worker of being a spy? Especially one who comes home for supper every day."

"You're right," Warren said. "Say, do you think he's spying for the Italians, for Mussolini?"

"Probably," Eddie answered. "Everyone around Seattle is always talking about Japanese spies. That's partly why they sent the Wakamutsus off to that camp. But unlike the Japanese, an Italian doesn't look any different from other white people, so that makes Sal a perfect spy."

"Sal, a spy! What are you talking about?"

"Barb! What are you doing sneaking up on us and eaves-dropping?" Eddie demanded of his twin.

"I didn't sneak," Barb said indignantly. "I walked right up to you, and you weren't talking low or anything."

"Anyhow it's a private conversation," Eddie said and turned as if to dismiss his sister.

Barb ignored his action and planted herself in front of the two boys. "Why do you think Sal is a spy? That sounds kind of crazy."

"We have our reasons," Eddie replied. He wasn't about to tell Barb about everything. The time for that would be after he and Warren had caught Sal in the act.

"He's not a very friendly guy," Barb conceded. "Most of the time he comes and goes by the fire escape door so he won't have to talk to anyone, but that doesn't make him a spy. You two are nuts."

Eddie gave Warren a quick look. Sal came and went by the fire escape door. That would explain why they could never catch him going through the lobby. Warren grinned a little, and

Eddie knew that he had caught on, too.

"You're right," Eddie said, "we're nuts." He felt like shouting now that they had something to go on, a clue given them by Barb, but he still didn't intend to spill the beans to her.

Carolyn came through the hotel front door just then, and Barb ran over to her. "You won't believe this," Barb said. "The boys think Sal is a spy."

"Let's get out of here before they start asking more questions," Eddie said. The two boys slipped away and down the hall toward Mr. Lazarini's apartment.

"Why didn't we think of the fire escape?" Warren asked. They stopped in front of the door in question.

"We would have eventually," Eddie said. He opened the door and looked down at the metal stairs that led to the alley. Sal could come and go all he pleased and not be noticed.

"Maybe not in time," Warren said. "Barb might have other ideas. Don't you think we should ask her and Carolyn, too?" He peered over Eddie's shoulder at the stairs.

"No," Eddie answered, "we don't need their help." After all, it was just an accident that Barb mentioned the fire escape. She didn't even know that it was important.

"What's next?" Warren asked with a shrug.

"We have to follow Sal," Eddie said and shut the fire escape door. "He should be home from work early for supper. I heard Mr. Lazarini say that Sal was working a shorter shift this week because of supply problems, and we know he never misses a meal. After that he must go to his place in the underground. We'll be watching the fire escape. From there we trail him and see what we can see."

The boys made their plans and went off to set them in

motion. They borrowed Frank's flashlight, and a couple hours later hid behind the trash cans in the alley and waited. Right on schedule Sal came walking down the alley, climbed the fire escape stairs, and disappeared inside. A half-hour later he reappeared, still dressed in his work clothes, carrying something wrapped in a white towel.

The boys waited until Sal was almost out of sight before following. They already knew he would head toward the underground. As soon as they could get lost in the people on the sidewalks, they closed the gap between themselves and Sal. It wasn't far to the downtown area where the long hidden underground passages snaked beneath the streets. Eddie knew that there were many vacant buildings among the businesses near the waterfront. He guessed that Sal had his operation set up below street level in one of the abandoned buildings that opened onto the lower, underground level. It would be a perfect place for a spy.

The boys kept close to the buildings they passed just in case Sal should turn around for any reason and they should need to duck inside. The businesses down here weren't ordinary grocery and clothing and hardware stores. Eddie knew that this part of Seattle was the rougher part of town with people and establishments to match. Even so, no one bothered the boys as they made their way closer to the waterfront.

First Sal was in plain sight, and then he wasn't. Eddie and Warren looked at each other and all around. Cautiously they approached the spot where they had last seen him, but there was no sign of the man.

"Where did he go?" Warren hissed in Eddie's ear.

"He's done his disappearing act again," Eddie said. He

scanned the street and sidewalks, looking for any clue. He turned to the nearest building, peering in the window of a door that opened onto the street.

"See anything?" Warren asked and crowded up behind Eddie.

"Maybe," Eddie said and opened the door. "Look," he said triumphantly. He pointed at a rickety wooden staircase that led down. "He must have gone down here."

Warren looked down the stairs. "It's dark."

"There's some light," Eddie said. "It must come from other openings like this one."

"Looks pretty dark to me," Warren said.

"Your eyes will get used to it," Eddie said. "Come on, we're going to lose him." He started down the staircase.

They found themselves in an area that looked and felt like a cave. Eddie sniffed at the musty-smelling air. There was a walkway of sorts that led off in the distance to another staircase. A wooden railing that had fallen down in places outlined the walkway. Off to the sides of the walkway was dusty debris of all kinds. With the flashlight Eddie could make out broken furniture scattered across the ground. Boards and piles of bricks were everywhere. On one side of the underground passage were doors and sometimes windows. It looked odd to see them, but Eddie realized that they opened onto a lower level of the existing buildings that had entrances above. He knew from the stories he had heard that the city had rebuilt the streets in this part of town after a fire many years ago. It was perfect for a spy's lair.

Eddie led the way as quickly and quietly as possible. They had already lost valuable minutes when Sal might even have climbed back up another of the staircases. Eddie strained his eyes ahead. Then he saw it. There was a tiny flutter of white that reflected back the light from an opening overhead. It had to be the napkin that Sal had wrapped around whatever he was carrying when he left the hotel.

"There he is," Eddie whispered to Warren and pointed.

"Let's get him," Warren whispered back. The boys hurried along the walkway, following the occasional glimpse of white ahead of them. It wasn't totally silent down here as it might be in a real cave. Eddie could hear traffic noises overhead and occasionally voices. He was thankful for that because it kept this tomb of a place from being quite as scary, and it helped mask any sound they might make as they chased Sal.

After what must have been a couple of blocks at least, a thud sounded up ahead. "He's gone in a door," Eddie said.

"Which one?" Warren craned his neck to look.

"It has to be this one," Eddie said as they came opposite a big wooden door. The walkway railing in front of that building had been pushed down, and the debris showed dim footprints where someone had walked up to the old door more than once.

"Why didn't he use these stairs?" Warren asked and waved at the staircase a few steps away. Light from the opening filtered down and offered a fairly clear view of the area near the door and the stairs.

"He didn't want anyone to trace him to this particular spot." Eddie walked over to the door.

"Smart guy," Warren said.

"Not so smart," Eddie said. "Because we're going to catch him." He tried the knob on the door, but it didn't move. "He locked it."

"Not good," Warren said. "Is there another way to get in?"

The boys backed up a step or two to look at the front of the underground building.

"Is that a window over there?" Warren asked.

Eddie looked where his friend pointed. A tiny opening was almost hidden under a beam that supported the sidewalk above. "Good eyes, pal. Let's see if we can get in."

The window was very small, but the wooden shutter that had covered it drooped from the sash. Eddie pulled the shutter, and it fell to the ground. The window was only a few feet off the ground, so he stuck the flashlight in and looked around. He saw an entryway cluttered with broken chairs and an old table.

Eddie pulled his head back out. "He went in this way. I'd bet on it." Eddie frowned at the window. It was so small. "Let's see if we can make this opening bigger."

They clawed at the frame around the window and managed to break off a piece or two. "Now," Eddie said. "Let me try it." He stuck his head in again and tried to wiggle his shoulders through the opening. "Push!"

Warren pushed, but Eddie's shoulders just rammed painfully into what was left of the window frame. "Wait!" He pulled back and rubbed his shoulders. "It's still too small."

"Maybe I can make it," Warren said and stuck his head in. It was immediately clear that his shoulders were even broader. "Sorry," he said. "Won't work."

"There must be some way to make this bigger," Eddie said and pulled some more at the window, but the old building was brick and wouldn't give another inch. At last he stopped to rub his scraped knuckles.

"What now?" Warren asked as they both stood, staring at the window.

"I don't know," Eddie answered. He fought the frustration that welled up inside him. They were so close, and time was running out. In hours it would be Saturday, the day that Sal was to have the goods. After that, time might run out for other people if Sal really was a spy—people like Dad and Isabel who worked so hard making the airplanes that helped Steve and the other soldiers fight the war.

A loud sneeze interrupted Eddie's thoughts with a jolt. He whipped around. What now? Had someone caught them spying as they tried to catch a spy themselves? He could see nothing in the dim passageway behind them. Then it came again, sneezing, only this time there were two sneezes in quick succession. They came from near the stairs.

"Who's there?" Eddie called out boldly. He wasn't feeling quite as brave as he made his voice sound, and he could tell by Warren's face that he was scared, too.

There was no answer, but another sneeze burst out of the darkness. Eddie frowned. Something about that sneeze was familiar, but he couldn't quite think what. It was enough to give him courage, and he walked quickly across the dusty debris to the stairs.

"I said, who's there!"

Four eyes stared back at him.

CHAPTER 12

Time Runs Out

"Hi," Barb said weakly and raised her hand in greeting. The other two eyes belonged to Carolyn.

"What are you doing here?" Eddie demanded

"I might ask you the same thing," Barb said and walked out from behind the stairs. "Does Mama know you're off down here in the underground?"

"Does she know where you are?"

The twins glared at each other for a moment before Carolyn spoke up. "Knock it off, you two. None of us should be down here. But we are, so out with the story, Eddie."

Eddie wasn't used to Carolyn being so forceful. It took him by surprise, and he blurted out, "We're following Sal."

"That's pretty clear," Barb said. "We saw you follow him from the hotel. That's why we followed you. But why? Does this have something to do with that spy idea of yours?"

"It's not just a crazy idea. We've got to stop him before tomorrow," Eddie said.

"Stop him from what?" Barb asked.

"It's nothing you need to know about. It's too dangerous for girls. Right, Warren?" Eddie turned to his friend.

Warren stared at Eddie. Finally Warren answered, "I suppose so."

Eddie expected Barb to blow up, but she didn't. Instead she looked thoughtfully at the window behind the boys. "So you want to get inside that window?"

Eddie nodded. "To unlock the door. That's why you two better get out of here and let us get back to work."

"I don't think so," Barb said with a grin. "I think you need us."

"What are you talking about?" Warren asked.

"I can get through that window and open the door," Barb said and walked over to the small opening.

"No you can't," Eddie said. Even as he said it, he knew that tiny Barb could probably squirm right through that opening.

"Sure I can." Barb grabbed a discarded wooden box that was nearby, climbed up on it, and stuck the whole top part of her body through the window.

"Fine," Eddie said impatiently. "Get in there and unlock the door."

"Not so fast," Barb said and tapped her fingers on her chin. "First you have to promise you'll tell us what you know about Sal and this spy business."

Eddie started to protest.

"And," Barb continued, "you have to let us go along."

"That's no fair," Eddie said. "We want to do this by ourselves."

"Take it or leave it," Barb said and waited.

"Eddie," Warren said and grabbed his friend's arm to pull him aside. "This is no time to work alone just to beat the girls. She's right. We need her, and who knows, we may need both of them before this is over."

Eddie frowned at his friend for a moment, but he knew Warren was right.

What was he thinking? This was about more than beating Barb at one of their silly contests. Lives might be at stake. They'd have to work together to stop Sal.

"Get in there," Eddie said. "We don't have a lot of time."

Barb grinned and nodded at her brother. "I need some help. I'm not going headfirst through that window. Help me get my feet through first."

Warren and Eddie held Barb up by the arms while she stuck her feet through the window. With a wiggle or two, the rest of her body followed, and she disappeared inside the building with the flashlight they handed through the opening. In moments they heard her at the big door, where she threw a bolt and pushed the door open.

"So tell us," Barb said as she stepped into the passageway. "And make it snappy." Dirt was smeared across her face and down her shirt.

Eddie gave the girls a quick rundown of events, with

Warren adding a detail here and there. "And the tall man said tomorrow was the day," Eddie said. "The day that Sal has to deliver the goods."

Barb's eyes were large in her small face. "So you're not crazy. He is a spy. Why are we standing here? There's work to be done, spy-catching work."

Eddie scanned the entryway with the flashlight. It was small and led to a large room on one side and a staircase on the other. Everything was dark and quiet in the large room, so they started up the stairs. Cobwebs brushed Eddie's face once, but he pushed them away and kept going. At the top of the stairs was a long hallway with many doors. The stairs were in the middle of the hall.

"Which way?" Warren asked from behind Eddie, who was in the lead.

Eddie listened for a moment, but all he could hear was the distant sound of car horns honking on the street. Which way led to Sal's hideout? He leaned down to shine the flashlight on the floor. Footprints in the thick dust led off to the right, while in the other direction, the dust was smooth.

"This way," he whispered and turned to the right, moving cautiously down the hall. As each door loomed in front of them, they stopped and listened. Each time Eddie shook his head as they heard nothing and walked on. Once Barb cautiously opened one of the doors to find a jumble of old furniture and junk.

At last the hallway turned, and all four peeked around the corner before proceeding. There was light up ahead. Eddie guessed it was the late afternoon sun shining in through big windows. They pressed themselves close against the side of the hall and moved toward the light. Eddie heard a rhythmic thudding, faint at first, but growing louder as they went forward. It was an odd sound. He could tell by their faces that the others were mystified as well.

What could a spy do that would cause a sound like that? Eddie and the others found themselves at the edge of a huge lobby with doorways all around. There was no sign of Sal or anyone else. The lobby floor was littered with trash. The thudding sound was quite loud now, but it didn't come from the lobby. It seemed to come from above a grand open staircase that rose in the center of the lobby. The railings were carved wood and bordered wide steps. Eddie looked up. The staircase split in two about halfway up. Each narrower staircase curved outward and led to another floor.

Eddie was distracted for just a moment by the grandeur he saw. What a sight this room must have been in the old days. A shove from Barb brought him back to the present. The odd sound still throbbed and thumped. It definitely came from above. He jerked his head in that direction and started up the stairs. The others followed without a word.

He hesitated a moment at the split in the stairway and turned right. The sound had grown louder. At the top of the stairs was yet another hallway, but this time light from an open doorway lit the way. The rhythmic sound pulsed from the room, and now he could hear another background sound that might be a motor. What was going on?

The four friends circled the pool of light that poured out into the dark hallway and tiptoed up to stand against the wall by the open door. Just as Eddie was ready to peek around the door's edge, the thudding sound stopped. A few seconds later the motor stopped, too. All was silent. Eddie's heart pounded until he thought whoever was inside that room could surely hear it.

They waited, pressed against the wall, listening. A voice said something from a distance. Eddie couldn't make out what was said, but he breathed once again. The voice was nowhere near. Then he heard another voice, equally distant. He listened for a moment and steeled himself to lean out for a quick look.

The room was almost as large as the Harringtons' whole apartment and was lit by several lanterns. There were no windows. A row of boxes was stacked across one end of the room. On the far side of the room were some tables with more boxes. Eddie didn't see any radio equipment, but he did see Sal. The chubby man stood near another man who Eddie didn't recognize. That man sat at one of the tables bent over something. Two lanterns glowed on either side of him. It looked like he was writing or drawing, but Eddie couldn't tell for sure.

"It's not good enough," Sal said loudly. "You'll have to do better than that. Look at this batch. I'm not paying you until you get it right."

Eddie retreated. What was Sal talking about? Was this the man from Number Two, the one Sal had mentioned persuading? Eddie leaned around the door again. Sal was eating something. Occasionally he wiped his hands on a white cloth. It was the towel that had led them to the door in the passageway. Sal was eating while he betrayed his country. Anger flooded over Eddie. He wanted to get this guy. He motioned for the others to step back down the hall.

They held a whispered conference.

"We have to try to get closer," Eddie said. "I can't see enough from here to tell what he's doing."

"Let's go inside then," Barb said. "We'll sneak behind those boxes you saw."

"It's risky," Eddie said.

Barb shrugged. "We can't let Sal get away with this, but we have to have some kind of proof, at least a closer look at what they're doing."

Eddie sighed. Barb was right as usual. "We'll have to be quiet as mice. If they turn that machine back on, whatever it was, that will help, but we can't be sure they'll turn it back on."

One by one, the four friends slipped into the room and crouched behind the boxes. Eddie led the way as they moved a foot at a time closer to Sal and the other man. The row of boxes led very close to the table where the man still sat.

"I'm going to give this plate another try," Sal said. "It still might work, but you keep going on that one."

In a moment a motor put-putted to life, and a few seconds later the thudding sound filled the room again. It sounded like something hitting something else, not hard, but hitting nonetheless. Eddie looked at Barb and the others as they crouched behind the boxes. He was sure now about the motor, but what was that other noise?

Carolyn sat up straighter and tilted her head. In the dim light, Eddie saw her face tense as she listened. Suddenly she smiled and nodded to herself. She motioned for the others to put their heads close. "It's a printing press," she said.

A printing press! Eddie sat back on his heels. What was a

spy doing with a printing press? It didn't make sense. He put his mouth up to Carolyn's ear. "Are you sure?"

Carolyn nodded firmly. "One of my uncles had a print shop before the war. That's what a printing press sounds like. I was just too scared to recognize it before."

The noise continued to thud. Eddie raised up enough to peek over the top of the boxes. Sal stood over a machine that Eddie hadn't noticed before. A printing press, no doubt.

The foursome edged closer to the far end of the boxes, which were barely stacked taller than their heads as they crawled. The noisy press covered any sounds they might make. At last they stopped. Any further advance would have to be across the open floor, an open floor that was littered with pieces of paper. Eddie studied the litter that covered the floor. What was that? Several pieces lay just out of his reach. He peeked around the edge of the last box and waited until he saw Sal turn away. Quickly he leaned out to grab one of the crumpled slips of paper.

The press continued to pound as he crouched back down behind the boxes and smoothed the paper while the others watched. It was printed with red ink and looked familiar, although the printing was too blurred to read easily.

Barb grabbed the paper. "It's the front of a ration coupon book." She handed it to Carolyn.

"But why is he printing. . ." Eddie began. He looked at Barb, and she slowly nodded. "He's not a spy, he's a counterfeiter," Eddie said.

"He's making ration books to sell on the black market," Barb said.

"That's almost as bad as being a spy," Warren said. Warren's words were said in a low voice but seemed suddenly loud because the press stopped just as he said them. His voice pierced the silence like an arrow.

"Who's that!" Sal shouted. "I heard someone, Henry. Quick, look over there." Sal stumbled over a chair as he lurched toward the boxes.

"Run!" Eddie yelled.

Eddie pulled at Barb's arm while Warren and Carolyn scrambled up to flee. In a flash they were around the boxes and out the door. They pounded down the grand stairs.

"Hey, you kids! Stop right now!" Sal yelled, but Eddie heard him puffing as he ran.

As Eddie reached the bottom of the stairs, he glanced back. Sal was behind them, but there was no sign of the other man, the one Sal called Henry. The big lobby was almost dark now, the setting sun leaving only a glow in the west. It would be even darker in the hallway because Eddie had dropped the flashlight in his haste to run. At least Sal wouldn't have a light, either.

Sal had fallen behind on the stairs. Eddie could hear him cursing as he stopped to rest for a moment. Too many rich meals had made Sal too plump for his own good. That was a lucky break.

They ran down the middle of the dark hallway and reached the top of the last set of stairs. Eddie saw Barb fling open a nearby door. What was she doing? This was no time to be sightseeing. She dragged something out of the room and put it at the top of the stairs. It was a bench of some sort.

"That'll fix him," she said.

Eddie grabbed her arm again as they climbed over the

bench and felt their way down the dark stairs. The damp smell of the underground passage came up to meet them. But now that smell meant escape. Again they felt their way across the entryway of the building and stumbled out into the passageway. A single beam of light shone from near the staircase where Barb and Carolyn had hidden earlier. There must be a street light right above. Eddie looked at the beam. Or maybe God had sent a light to guide them. Whatever the source, the beam would steer them out of the darkness that pressed all around.

Before they could move, there was a loud clattering behind them followed by an equally loud string of curses, courtesy of Sal. Eddie chuckled. Their would-be spy had found the bench Barb had left for him. If the anger in his voice was any guide, Sal wasn't seriously hurt, but his accident bought them time.

Warren led the way, and the other three followed as they climbed the stairs. Fresh air had never smelled so good to Eddie. They ran down the street a little way before stopping near a brightly lit corner.

"I can't believe Sal is a counterfeiter," Warren said.

"Instead of a spy," Barb said with a grin at her brother.

"The pieces all fit," Eddie said. "I just had the wrong puzzle."

"I would have thought the same thing," Barb said.

"But how are we going to blow the whistle on him?" Warren said. "Will anyone believe us? It is a pretty crazy story."

"Oh, they'll believe us," Carolyn said. "We have proof."

The other three looked at her, puzzled, until she pulled a piece of paper out of her pocket. It was the crumpled front of the counterfeit ration book that they had looked at earlier.

They cheered before turning toward home and the long explanations that would follow.

CHAPTER 13

Winners

The hotel buzzed with the news of Sal's counterfeiting for the next few days. Everyone had an opinion and wasn't afraid to express it. Mr. Lazarini was very upset by his relative's crime and the way it made Italian Americans look. Eddie was glad to see that almost every person in the hotel made it a point to tell Mr. Lazarini that they knew it was no reflection on him that he had a crook for a cousin.

Sal had disappeared once more, but the police had confiscated his printing press and said they had several leads on finding him. The tall man and the woman in black had been brought in for questioning about a big black market ring that was operating in the Seattle area. They had been picked up Saturday as they tried to enter Sal's hideout.

Sal had been working the black market for months, illegally selling ration coupons that he stole or bought at a low price. He had been trying to set up his counterfeit operation for some time but lacked a good engraver to make the metal plates for printing the coupons. The man he called Henry had been his latest employee. Henry was nowhere to be found, either.

Eddie realized that Sal's interest in Boeing hadn't been so he could pass on information to the enemy, but rather to help him figure out how to get his racket going.

It was an exciting time for Eddie and Barb. Mama took turns scolding them for trying to catch a spy alone and praising them for working together at last. Eddie had to take a little teasing over the spy thing, especially from Frank and his older sisters. It helped that Barb didn't rub it in that he had mistaken a counterfeiter for a spy.

The first week of June had been one to remember. The following Tuesday Eddie was thinking about everything that had happened as he walked home from the Victory garden. It was his day to pull weeds and carry some water to the tomatoes if they needed it. He was also thinking about the scrap drive that he and Warren still hoped to win, along with Carolyn and Barb.

It hadn't really been hard at all to ask the girls to share the scrap from the car. Carolyn's father was helping them work out all the details before he hauled the junk car to the collecting station. It wasn't boys against the girls any longer. Catching Sal had taught Eddie that working together gets the job done better. Not that he intended to tell Barb that anytime soon.

There was a stir in the barber shop as he neared the corner. Several people were talking at once. Someone ran out of the barber shop and yelled to no one in particular, "It's started." Eddie slowed his walk and looked in the window. Five men and a woman stood bunched up near the counter, and others hurried in from the street. What was happening?

The crackling of radio static filled the air briefly. The barber had his radio on the counter with the volume turned up. The people inside the shop quieted. Eddie hurried inside with the others. An announcer came on and said that in a few moments, his station would broadcast a live announcement by an army public information officer. More static followed, and then a steady voice said, "Under the command of General Eisenhower, Allied naval forces supported by strong air forces began landing Allied armies this morning on the northern coast of France." A cheer rose in the barber shop.

Eddie backed away and ran out the door. He wanted to get home and tell his family. The invasion of Europe had begun!

The mood in the hotel varied from jubilation that the war might soon be over to fear for the soldiers who had undertaken such a task. Mama's face paled when she heard the news. Eddie saw her close her eyes for a few seconds, and he knew she was praying for Steve and the others. But then she opened them and smiled, ready to share in the excitement.

There was no news about Steve's part in the invasion, if indeed he had been one of the soldiers splashing ashore on the beaches of France. A few hours later, Eddie and Barb and the others listened as the famous war correspondent, Edward R.

Murrow, reported from London. He said that the bombers going out made the sound of a giant factory in the sky.

Dad said that this was another time when no news was probably good news when it came to Steve. Each day that passed without a telegram arriving lifted Eddie's spirits a little higher.

At last it was the day of the war bond rally. Carolyn's father had towed the old car to the collection center, and the four friends had made sure that the weight was carefully recorded so they would get proper credit. The winner of the scrap-collecting contest was to be announced at the rally.

"Hurry up," Eddie said to Barb. The rally was due to start in an hour, and Barb was still finishing her chores. For once Eddie had beaten his sister, and he hadn't even been trying.

"There, I'm done," Barb said and shoved her dust mop back in the closet. "I'll just wash my hands, and we can go." She ran down the hall toward their apartment.

Eddie groaned. He and Barb were supposed to meet Warren and Carolyn at Victory Square in ten minutes. It wasn't far, but Eddie didn't want to be late.

"Why the rush?" Barb asked a few minutes later as Eddie hurried her toward downtown. "They won't announce the winner right away. There are always speeches. You know that."

"I heard there might be famous people there," Eddie said. "I thought we should be early so we can get up front."

"Like who?"

"Movie stars, maybe," Eddie answered. "It probably was just a rumor. In fact, I'm sure it was a rumor. Forget I said that."

"What are you so nervous about?" Barb asked as they turned the last corner before Victory Square. "Which movie star was it, anyhow?"

Eddie pretended not to hear his sister. "There's Warren and Carolyn." He waved at their friends.

"Did you tell Barb about Lana Turner?" Warren asked as soon as the twins walked up.

Eddie frowned at Warren and shook his head slightly, but it was too late.

"Lana Turner!" Barb said. "So that's the movie star. Why didn't you just say it was her?"

"It may be just a rumor," Eddie said.

Carolyn laughed and gave Eddie a knowing look. "Maybe he doesn't want us to know that he's sweet on Lana Turner."

"That must be right," Barb said. "How about it, twin brother?"

"Am not!" Eddie said loudly.

"Am too!" Barb said.

"No arguing," Warren said, "at least not over the lovely Lana."

"Come on," Eddie said. "Forget that. Let's get a good place to stand."

"So we can be close to the front when we win the scrap contest," Carolyn said.

Lana Turner forgotten, the friends staked out a spot and waited for the rally to begin. It was like the other rallies that Eddie had attended before. There were speeches and music and lots of joking around by the people in charge. And always there was the plea for people to buy war bonds and stamps to help pay for the war. Eddie kept his eyes peeled, but he didn't see any sign of Lana Turner. It would almost be worth the teasing to get to see the movie star in person. He knew that she and lots of other celebrities went all around the country appearing at rallies, but it looked like she wasn't coming to this one.

Finally it was time to announce the winner of the scrap-collecting contest but, as usual, the master of ceremonies liked to take his time in order to build up suspense. He told stories and jokes, which sometimes made the audience groan.

"Now, the moment you've been waiting for," he said, and the crowd cheered. Eddie and the others strained forward. An assistant hurried on stage with a note that the MC read before turning back for a whispered consultation with some other people on stage.

The MC motioned toward the edge of the stage before turning to the audience to announce, "We have an unexpected guest who will be coming aboard to help with the award."

There was a stir offstage. A gasp rose from the crowd as the guest walked across the stage. Eddie's eyes widened. It was Lana Turner!

The movie star moved gracefully toward the microphone, waving and smiling to the crowd, which had found its voice and now cheered loudly. She spoke briefly about the importance of buying bonds, but Eddie didn't hear a word. He was too busy looking at the star.

"And now," the MC said, "Miss Turner will award the scrap metal—collecting prize."

Eddie and Warren stared at each other for a moment. Would they get the prize from the hands of a famous movie star? Eddie wiped his sweaty hands on his pants just in case.

The same assistant hurried across the stage to hand the MC a note. Again, he read it and paused for a conference before turning back to his microphone. "We have another entry in the contest that we want to show you. I think he'll be coming right through there." The MC pointed to the back of the crowd. Sure enough. A flurry of movement began at the edge of the square.

Everyone shuffled and leaned and craned their necks to get a better look. Eddie and Warren climbed up on a nearby bench.

"What do you see?" Barb demanded.

"It looks like a team of horses pulling something," Warren reported.

"What is it?" Eddie asked.

About that time the crowd parted to let the horses through. A boy about Eddie's age walked alongside an older man. Eddie couldn't see what the horses pulled but could hear scraping and crunching as it moved along the street. Then the crowd moved once more, allowing him a clear view. "Why, it's a steamroller. At least it's the roller off a steamroller. It's huge."

"And made of metal, no doubt," Barb said.

"Solid iron," Warren said with a knowing nod.

Eddie sighed and jumped down from the bench. Warren followed him. The crowd laughed and cheered at the sight of a big iron roller being towed in by horses.

"It'll weigh a ton," Barb said.

"More than that," Eddie said.

"More than our car?" Carolyn asked as she looked from Eddie to Warren to Barb.

"Lots more," Warren said and turned to grin at Eddie. "No Lana Turner handshake for us."

"I bet he was hoping for a kiss," Barb teased.

"Was not!" Eddie said and blushed bright red.

"We didn't win the contest," Barb said, "but we did get a

lot of scrap metal for the war effort."

"Winning the war is the only contest that matters," Eddie said. The others nodded, and they all pushed through the crowd to see the lucky guy who would get his award from Lana Turner.

There's More

The American Adventure continues with *Coming Home*. Eddie can't move, and Barb is terrified that something is wrong with him. Sure enough, when the doctor meets Eddie at the hospital, he simply shakes his head and puts Eddie in a special ward. Will Eddie ever walk again?

As Barb and Eddie adjust to his illness, news of heavy fighting in Europe raises new concerns. Will their older brother Steve survive these horrible battles? And will they ever learn what happened to their sister's fiancé, Jim Watson? When the war is over, who will be coming home?